JAZZ GIRL

A Novel of
Mary Lou Williams
And Her Early Life

Sarah Bruce Kelly

Bel Canto Press

www.belcantopress.com

ISBN   978-0-615-35376-0

Cover Art: Piano Jazz Plant, serigraph,
by Maria Termini

To Frank, Frankie, and Mary Catherine,
the loves of my life,
and to Mary Lou Williams,
who shared her love with so many
through her music

"Jazz created for all people.

Jazz created through suffering.

Got beaten everyday.

And school—Amy Frank."

~ Mary Lou Williams

1910-1981

Prologue

The Sign of the Caul

Atlanta, Georgia 1910

"This baby girl been born with a veil over her eyes."

That's what the midwife told my mama the day I came into this world. The ghostly thing called the caul that covered my newborn face frightened my mama. "I reckon she be strange, then," Mama said. Least that's what she always told me she said. The caul went away but the gift it signified never did.

The midwife said the caul meant I came with the gift of second sight and some people might think that's a good thing. But it's burdened me with a lot of troubles. For example I learned at an early age that my mama didn't love me. Truth was she couldn't abide my strangeness. It spooked her, I guess. When ghosts would visit me in the night and I'd run to Mama she never tried to comfort me. She tied me to the bed. And when I got so scared I'd stutter Mama would spit in my mouth to make me stop. The stuttering only got worse. So I stopped trying to talk altogether. This made Mama and just about all my other relations think I was even more peculiar than they had before.

And because I was so quiet and mopy my stepdaddy Winn would get great kicks out of tickling me till I almost had a spasm. One night after I'd screamed and screamed for mercy from the tickling I dreamed he was smothered by sand. Then he died at the laboring yard where he worked when a truck dumped a load of gravel on him.

That's when I knew the "sign of the caul," my special gift of seeing, was a powerful thing.

1

East Liberty

Pittsburgh, Pennsylvania 1922

"M-m-m-Mary!" a girl on the sidewalk shouted when I went outside to play. Her name was Amy Frank, the pretty little blond girl next door. She wasn't allowed to play with me but my sister Mamie whose skin was light could play with her. Amy was the belle of the neighborhood and a real bearcat besides. She'd look at me like I was no better than a gutter rat.

Amy and some other neighbor girls were playing jump rope on the sidewalk and I tried to join in. They didn't want me there because of my darkness and my stuttering.

"You dumbbell," one of the girls said, and everybody laughed.

When you stutter people think you're stupid. And I couldn't tell these girls any different 'cause the words would just come out as more stutter. I felt the burning wetness press against the backs of my eyes but I didn't let the tears get to the outside parts of my eyes. I didn't want Amy and the other girls to see me cry.

My family and me'd just moved to Pittsburgh the week before. We came by railroad which was real thrilling because it was my first train ride. The rhythm of the engine and sounds of the horn and bells was like music to my ears. The noises put me in mind of the train that hooked up the colored and white parts of town back home in Atlanta. I figured maybe this train connecting Atlanta and Pittsburgh would carry me to a different world where people wouldn't be so separate.

We must've looked a sight when we got off at the station what with all the trunks and bags tied with ropes. There was me and Mama, my big sister Mamie, my grandma who I called Nanny, and Grandpa. It was Nanny who agitated to get the family out of Georgia and go up north where things were supposed to be evened out between colored and white folks. So we traded Atlanta's warm magnolia smelling breezes for the cold smoky air of Pittsburgh.

We settled in a neighborhood called East Liberty.

Our little wooden whitewashed house on Hamilton Avenue was newly built with a modern day kitchen and inside bathroom. Since it was near Christmas I wasn't starting up at my new school till after the New Year. I figured that'd give me lots of time to make friends with the neighbor girls. But they didn't want to be friends with the likes of me.

After the girls on the sidewalk teased me about my stuttering I ran back in the house and peered through the window. Those pretty white girls were laughing and playing Double Dutch with their jump ropes and having a fine time. I wanted to be like those girls.

But I couldn't. I could only be myself with my dark skin and peculiar ways. And my music. That's what saved me from misery. The music inside me gave me so much joy I thought I'd bust if it didn't get out. Problem was I had no piano or organ to practice my music on and my fingers were itching to play. All I could do was hum or sing to myself. But like my Nanny always said my singing sounded more like the night squalling of an old alley cat. So most times the music stayed inside my head, leaping and dancing around like the spirits who used to play with me in the Georgia woods around our old house.

Back in Atlanta I spent most of my time at the store-front church where my mama played the pump organ on Sunday mornings. She'd go there every day to practice and always took me with her. First I tried to copy things I heard Mama play. Then I started playing my own music, the music that was in my head. It wasn't long before Mama let me go to the church on my own to practice. Got me out from underfoot she said. I got lots of grumbly stares for this from the neighbors since a girl's supposed to stay home and help her mama in the kitchen.

But I never got close to my mama and never wanted to be like her. She put the love of music in my heart but she also taught me hearts can be very cold. Hers sure was. So instead of clamoring for hugs from Mama I pestered her to let me go down the street to the church every day so I could play the organ.

Only problem was my scrawny legs were too short to reach the pedals. So I asked the minister's boy to get down on his hands and knees and do the pumping which he did gladly because of the feeling of importance it gave him. Till he got tired. Then I had to slide down far as I could to get my feet to the pumping pedals and reach my hands practically above my head to play the organ keys. Not the best way to play. But my little heart was aching so bad to get the music out I'd do anything to make it happen. Even stretch out my arms and legs like Jesus on the cross if I had to.

2

The Ghost Dog

Soon as I walked in the house a familiar smell put Amy Frank and the other neighbor girls clear out of my mind. I ran to the kitchen. Nanny'd put ham hocks and onions to boiling on the stove and was setting to clean the chitlins. The delicious smells set my belly to rumbling and put me in mind of back home and the stories Nanny used to tell around the supper table.

Nanny's stories were mostly fearsome tales about ghosts and spooks. The same ghosts and spooks that were in my visions and mixed up with music in my head. The story that scared me most was the one about the Ghost Dog.

While Nanny scrubbed the chitlins in a bowl of water and cut away their fat I begged her to tell me that story again. She sighed in a wearisome way but finally obliged as she most always did.

"Well child, I be snapping beans in the kitchen one evening long ago when I heard a clattering on the front porch and the sound of a child screaming. I run to open the door to find the little boy from down the road shaking and blubbering. 'Keep that thing from gettin' me!' he hollered."

Nanny asked him why he was so scared.

"I jus' saw the worst looking creature I ever seen in my life. I hope I won't never see such a sight again long as I live," the boy wailed.

Nanny wanted to know what foolish thing he'd seen.

"It weren't anything foolish. I been walking by them old gravestones long side the dirt road when I heard a noise. I looked around and saw the most terrible, biggest, whitest dog in the world. That dog was looking straight at me and I started galloping like crazy with the dog champin' at my heels. It stayed right behind me and never left till I turned up the road to your house and started hollerin'."

"The boy was shaking and dripping with sweat," Nanny said when she finished the story, her stout chest heaving with sighs at the memory. "And ever after that awful evening there were many more tales told of the dreadful Ghost Dog."

Nanny put the chitlins in the boiling pot alongside the ham hock and added garlic, thyme, and a bay leaf. The wonderful smells got me shaking and practically drooling with hunger. But the story Nanny just told gave me the worst shakes. That Ghost Dog was as real to me as the ham hocks and chitlins boiling on the stove. More than Nanny or anybody knew. I just had to tell her.

"I seen that Ghost Dog rise up out of the swamp, Nanny. And lots of other spooks too."

"That's 'cause our house was built on top of a sunken cemetery," my nanny said.

Actually our house back in Atlanta looked more sunken than the cemetery. It was a dinky old wood shack near swampy woods. The kind of house where if you shot a gun through the front door the bullet passed through all the rooms and into the backyard, likely ending up in the privy.

That house was haunted not only by ghosts but by rowdy weekend drinking sprees. Mama and Nanny were the only drinkers. Their drinking was understandable seeing as all week long they washed and ironed for white folks. My mama who was admired for her beauty and her dainty figure almost became a hunchback carrying all those white peoples' laundry on her back. She fretted about that 'cause she was vain about her looks. So come weekends her and Nanny lost themselves in the gin.

The drinking didn't let up when we moved north. Turned out Mama and Nanny still had to knuckle under to white folks for us to get by. They washed and ironed all day just like they did in Atlanta and that's how we got on, same as we always had. Only it was so cold.

The coldness of Pittsburgh chilled more than just my body. I felt like a stranger in my new neighborhood and even with my own family. It seemed up north my darkness compared to the rest of my family showed up more than it did down south. Truth was Mama and most of my relations except for Grandpa had always made me feel different and treated me like dirt because I was so dark. But I'd never felt such a powerful lonesomeness as I did when we moved to smoggy old Pittsburgh. My heart was homesick for the swampy Georgia woods where I used to play, with spirits prancing 'round me and music dancing in my head.

East Liberty was nothing like those Georgia woods. It was a peculiar place since by noon the sun would dim to an early night, seein' as it was blotted out by thick black smoke. The smoke was from the Pittsburgh steel mills where most of our neighbors worked. These new neighbors were mostly poor white folks. Some of them had come to America from far off places. There were also a few Negroes but they were all pale like my relatives.

The white and light-skinned colored kids treated me like I had the plague. They thought I was too dark to play with. Even their mamas acted hateful.

THE DAY AFTER THE JUMPROPING GIRLS teased me about my stuttering I decided to see if they'd let me join in their game of hopscotch. Just as their teasing started Amy Frank's mama came running out of the house with a butcher knife, screaming, "Get out of our sight, you black vermin! You don't belong here! Your own mama don't even know how you got started!"

One minute I saw Mrs. Frank coming at me with that knife and the next minute I saw the big white Ghost Dog charging at me, his long yellow fangs dripping with drool. My body was shaking so bad I couldn't hardly move. I thought for sure I was done for.

"Leave the child be," came a quiet but firm voice from behind me.

It was Grandpa. He'd just arrived from his work at the laboring yard and I ran to him. He put his arm around me in a protecting way, still eyeing Mrs. Frank with his steady look. Grandpa was a small man but imposing. When he spoke, which wasn't too often, people listened.

Mrs. Frank's knife-wagging fist dropped to her side.

She seemed all fuddled. "Well. . . I . . . that was right silly of me, wasn't it?" She laughed, kind of, more like a titter. "Here I was in my kitchen carving up a chicken when I hear a great commotion among the children. And I come running outside not even realizing I'm still holding on to this thing." Her eyes moved from Grandpa to me and her lips became more firmly set. "I'm right sorry if I scared you."

Truth was I was so scared my teeth were clanking.

Amy and the other kids stood there with their mouths hanging open. Some of their mothers who'd been peering out their windows came clattering out of their houses to shoo their children inside.

Grandpa looked hard at the little crowd gathered on the sidewalk. "You folks stop bullying my grandbaby, you hear? She done you no harm." He squeezed my shoulder and steered me away from all the staring eyes. "Let's walk a spell, child," he said.

He let go of my shoulder and I clutched his hand.

"Don't let ignorant people frighten you, Messy," he said.

That was Grandpa's special name for me, Messy. I never knew why.

"You're smarter than any of 'em," he said, "and don't ever let nobody tell you different."

"But when Mrs. Frank came at me with that butcher knife I had one of my fearful visions, Grandpa. I saw her turn into the Ghost Dog Nanny told me about, and her knife became a big white fang."

"Pay that Ghost Dog no mind, Messy. Your nanny's wicked to tell you tall tales like that."

"It's real to me, Grandpa," I said, clutching his hand all the harder. "I saw it before my very eyes."

"Your visions are nothing to fear, child, and neither are those fool white folks. If my pappy could overcome his fears, you surely can."

I could see Grandpa was fixing to tell me one of his stories. I leaned close to him and listened.

"Pappy'd tell me at the end of each day he be totin' his basket of cotton to the gin house in fear and trembling."

"The gin house," I said, "was that where they drank gin like Mama and Nanny?"

He frowned. Grandpa didn't hold with drunkenness. "No indeed, child. The gin house where the cotton gin be."

"Cotton gin? What's that?"

"Cotton gin's a wooden box with a crank on its side that splits up the cotton fiber from the seeds. Slaves called it white man's magic."

"Was it really magic?"

"No, child. Gin mean engine. It just be an invention with different parts that works together for a single purpose, like any machine."

"If it was only a machine then what was your pappy so fearful of?"

"Well, if his basket was to fall short in weight he knew he had suffering coming. As he'd say it, *the whippin' would follow the weighin'*."

I can't even tell you the feeling I had at that moment. My sorrow was like a dark pit deep inside me. I must've started shaking again 'cause Grandpa put his arm around me and held me close and chuckled real soft.

"It weren't all so bad, child. My pappy also tell me about the music. How when the sun just breaking across the fields the slaves would come from all directions singing and the fields a-ringing with their song. Hundreds of 'em lifting their voices like the heavenly host itself."

I gazed into his gentle brown eyes. I'd turned twelve in May and Grandpa was short for a man so my eyes met his almost direct.

"What would they sing, Grandpa?"

He wrinkled his brow and scratched his soft gray curls. "Let's see here, I seem to remember one that went like this:

> *This time tomorrow night*
> *Where will I be?*
> *I'll be gone, gone, gone*
> *O'er to Tennessee.*"

"But that's a sad song, Grandpa."

"At times the slaves sing this sorrowful because some of 'em knowed they gonna be sold away from their families."

My eyes got prickly wet and I hugged him with all my might and he gave me back my hug. Grandpa's arms around me felt strong and comforting. I could feel the steady beat of his heart, like a drumbeat, and I was filled with fear that one day his heart would stop, and I'd be all alone.

3

Daddy Fletcher

Mrs. Frank was right about one thing. My mama didn't know how I got started. Least she never told me if she did. So I didn't know who my real daddy was. Whoever he was he up and left before I was born. Probably never even knew I was coming. All I know is I was born when Mama was married to my stepdaddy Winn who died from the gravel and he always made it plain he was no relation to me. "You just some sort of dark weed," he'd say. "Lord only knows who you is or where you come from."

Some sort of dark weed stepdaddy Winn called me. That sounded like an ugly thing so I figured I must be ugly. I'm guessing the caul made me that way and that's why Mama didn't love me.

Sometimes I thought maybe the Ghost Dog that haunted me was stepdaddy Winn's spirit come back to torment me. I fretted about this till Grandpa set my mind to rest.

"Don't you pay no mind to what that no-count Winn say, child, 'cause he ain't blood. Ain't no relation to you, so he got no business ponderin' where you come from. 'Sides, he passed on to the other side, or wherever folks like him goes when they dies. You got no need to worry yourself about him."

"It's not just what stepdaddy Winn said, Grandpa. Most folks hate me 'cause I'm so dark. How'd I get to be so dark when everybody else in the family's more light brown or tan?"

"Folks come in all shades of color, child. No telling what shade we be born with."

What Grandpa said put me in mind of music. Music comes in all shades of color too. Only with music you don't see the colors, you hear them. My special gift of seeing was a hearing thing too. I called those hearing kinds of colors *sound* colors. And sound colors were everywhere. I could hear them in the trees when the birds sang and in the wind coming across the Allegheny River that flows through Pittsburgh. Oh how my fingers itched to turn those sound colors into real live music.

~ 21 ~

But we still had no piano in our house. Lots of our neighbors had pianos though. And the neighbor kids liked my sister Mamie who was sixteen and light-skinned and pretty. She didn't have weird visions like me either. I wished I could be like her then maybe the neighbor kids would like me. And maybe Mama would like me too if I wasn't so dark and peculiar. Maybe even love me.

MAMA DID FIND LOVE in her heart a few days after Mrs. Frank came at me with the butcher knife. Only not for me. Grandpa came home that evening with a fine looking young fellow. His light tannish skin and kindly smile seemed to glow. You'd think the Good Lord hisself had walked in our front door the way Mama went all doe-eyed.

"This here's Fletcher Burley, from the laboring yard," Grandpa said, in his usual quiet way.

Fletcher Burley took off his workman's hat and a lock of his curly brown hair fell into his eye. He raked it back with his free hand and grinned the biggest handsomest grin I ever saw in my life. "It's right kind of you folks to have me for supper," he said.

I have to admit my heart did a little flip.

Well Mama's must've done a big flip because in less than a week's time her and Fletcher Burley were married and he moved in with us. Just like that I had a new daddy. I called him Daddy Fletcher.

4

The Piano

"Can't nobody play music like Mary here," my sister Mamie bragged to the girls on the sidewalk. They looked at her all admiring but at me like they didn't believe it.

Well to prove it, the next day Amy asked me to come in her house while her mama was at the market. Me and the other kids followed as she pranced on in that house like a prize pony. She marched straight over to her little upright piano then turned and looked at me like she was making a dare.

I was scared as could be since I'd never played a real piano, only the pump organ at our church back in

Atlanta. But I couldn't let Mamie down. Then all the kids would think she's a liar.

My fingers had the shivers but I sat at that piano and played a spiritual Grandpa'd taught me. I let the words swimming in my head guide my fingers:

Beams of heaven as I go
Through this wilderness below
Guide my feet in peaceful ways
Turn my midnights into days.

"That's a colored song, isn't it?" Amy said when I was finished. I could tell by the way she said colored that the song didn't suit her one bit.

"It's a spiritual," I said, feeling more shivery and tongue-tied than ever. "A song colored folks used to sing during slavery."

"Hmmph!" Amy said with her nose scrunched like she was smelling something bad. "Figures somebody with skin as black as yours couldn't play anything but colored songs. You're nothing but trash, like my mother says."

Amy smiled her mean smile and the other kids started to laugh. All of a sudden I couldn't breathe.

I almost tripped over my feet trying to get to the door, my head ready to bust from all the tears pushing to get out. I felt like my heart had smashed into a million pieces. Those smashed pieces were like bits of broken glass that floated around in me pricking and poking and tearing me up inside.

Since we'd moved to Pittsburgh I oftentimes had that torn up feeling. When it came all I could do was try to sing back together all the broken pieces of my heart since I had no organ or piano. And now I couldn't play piano at the neighbor's houses anymore. I couldn't abide them gibing me about my darkness. Until I got my own piano I'd just have to *sing* out those feelings that sizzled inside me like fire spitting up from a stove.

Not that my singing was any good. Like Nanny always told me, when I sang I sounded like a cat yowling from a tin roof. My stuttering didn't help either. I guess that's part of the reason my singing was so bad. The words I'd sing got caught in my throat just like the words I tried to speak got caught on the tip of my tongue. The stuttering kept my words from coming out smooth and regular like other folks. My words were smooth and regular when I thought them in my head but when they came out of my mouth they were all broken into pieces. Like the broken pieces of my heart.

If only Mama was more loving toward me maybe the broken pieces wouldn't even be there in the first place. I wanted her loving so much that at times I'd do foolish things to get her to pay me some mind. Those foolish things got me into nothing but trouble. Like the time back in Atlanta when I cut the roses off Nanny's rose bushes by our back steps. I wanted to give the roses to Mama as a special surprise. Then maybe she'd see how much I loved her and she'd love me back. You'd think I'd done murder the way Nanny carried on. And Mama didn't even care. The roses meant nothing to her no matter if they were still on the bush or standing in a jelly jar as a gift from her daughter. But that's not what hurt so bad. What hurt so bad was that *I* meant nothing to her either. Least that's how she made me feel. Maybe she wanted to love me but just couldn't. Maybe that kind of loving, to love a daughter peculiar as me, wasn't in her.

My house was only a few steps from Amy's but my feet were dragging so slow 'cause of my gloomy thoughts it seemed like a mile. When I finally slunk in the front door Daddy Fletcher was already home from work. At the sight of him my feet got some life and I ran to him.

"That Amy Frank's the meanest girl in the world. She says I'm trash 'cause my skin's so dark." I buried my face in his blue workman's shirt and bawled.

"Don't pay that white miss no mind, Baby Doll. You got more talent in your little finger than that wicked girl's got in her whole dizzy little brain."

I sniffled and clung to him all the harder.

He patted my shoulder. "Now don't you worry none about it," he said. "What other folks says can't hurt you 'lessin you let it." Then he chuckled and pulled away from me. "Get me a ciggy, Baby Doll."

I wiped away my tears and gladly rushed to get him a cigarette and light. And I about fell over at the sight I beheld soon as the fog cleared from my eyes. Over in the far corner of the parlor sat a big tall wooden thing.

"A piano!" I squeaked, all of a sudden forgetting my torn up feelings.

"This isn't just any piano, Baby Doll," Daddy Fletcher said. "This here's a clever machine. It can work like a reg'lar one, but it also lets you hear the music of famous players by playing their piano rolls."

"Piano rolls? What are those, Daddy Fletcher?"

"Come here and let me show you, Baby Doll. Piano rolls are like magic. Each one holds a different song, played by the most famous piano players in the world. It's like having Jelly Roll Morton right here in our own parlor."

I was so excited my heart was bouncing like a pogo stick. We played roll after roll and watched the piano keys play themselves. Like a ghost was playing them. There were old ballads, waltzes, opera tunes, marches, ragtime—and a jumpy kind of music I'd never heard before.

"That jumpy music's called boogie," Daddy Fletcher said, flashing his big handsome grin.

I giggled at the funny name but my feet couldn't keep

from hopping 'round the room to the snappy beat.

The boogie and rags were my favorites. But I also loved a song by Jelly Roll Morton called "The Pearls" which wasn't perky like the boogie tunes but real smooth and pretty.

I learned to play the pearl song that very day by slowing down the piano roll and pressing my fingers to the keys as they played themselves. I did this over and over till I'd memorized the song, so I could play it myself.

EARLY NEXT MORNING I couldn't wait to get to my new piano. My very own piano! Now I could spend all day working things out and making my own sounds.

Before I could even get to the piano the sounds in my head got me jumping and hopping like a leapfrog which was a dangerous way to be in my house. That kind of acting up would likely get me a whipping from Mama since she didn't hold with much commotion from Mamie or me. Set her head to pounding she said. No wonder the way she slugged the gin night after night. You'd think Mama would be right tickled to be living in this fine new house with a fine new husband and she'd stop drinking so much. Her drinking didn't let up though.

I'm guessing the gin made her feel happy. Least for a little while. It also made her meaner than ever when the happy feeling wore off. Those were the times I had to be real careful about.

But today I was feeling too bubbly inside to be mindful as I should have been. I ran to Mama the minute she came out of her bedroom that morning and hopped up and down. "Look, Mama, look! Look at my new piano."

Mama didn't smile. She stared at me for a minute with a blank sort of look then turned away and went to the kitchen.

I followed her, itching to tell her about my excited feelings. "But, Mama, all my visions that get mixed up with music in my head are gonna turn into something real now. Something wonderful. I'm gonna make music that'll bring folks together. Music that'll turn their hearts."

"That be the devil playin' round in your head," she said while she poured herself some coffee with a shaky hand. "You best not be conjurin' up more of them visions like you done before."

"I don't mean to conjure visions," I said, my head hanging.

"You sure enough put folks in mind of spooks. Cursed you is, by the sign of the caul. All the time scarin' folks with your peculiar ways."

"Sorry, Mama," I said, and tears pricked my eyes. "I

don't mean to scare folks. But the feelings the visions give me are what go into making my music."

Mama drank her coffee and didn't say anything.

My eyes were stinging and I blinked a lot to dry the wetness. I'd poured out my heart to Mama and all she could say was my visions come from the devil 'cause I been cursed. My deep down feelings didn't matter to her one bit.

5

The Train Trestle

"Look at that child, all day at the piano," Nanny grumbled. "That all she do. Couldn't nobody hardly take her away from practicing. No wonder she so string bean thin. Never even stops to eat a decent meal."

"She's a rail, all right," Mama said. "To look at her folks would think we didn't feed her nothin'."

I went on with my piano playing but I could see Mama's look out the corner of my eye. It was the look that said I best watch out 'cause trouble sure be coming.

"Mary, you heard what your mama said. Now get yourself to the kitchen so's I can feed you something proper. Something that'll put some meat on your skinny little bones."

"Thank you kindly, Nanny, but I'm not hungry. I best get on with my practicing."

Nanny shook her head in her disapproving way. Mama went to the kitchen and I heard the gin bottle pop open. My stomach got snarly and sick feeling. After a time Nanny went to join Mama. I kept on with my playing and tried not to think about what was going on in that kitchen. The drinking made me sad, mostly because it kept Grandpa in the basement where he went to get away from the boozing. I wanted him in the parlor sharing in my music making.

Was that how it had to be? I wondered. Mama's drinking keeping us apart? Used to be the whole family'd gather round the kitchen table come supper time. Truth was Nanny didn't have much time for cooking nowadays 'cause of the laundry business she and Mama set up in our new house the day after we moved in. But lately the laundry business hadn't been doing too good. The reason was likely that partying soon took over.

First couple weeks they'd only brought out the jugs on Fridays after the washing was done. But come near Christmas they were drinking all day and hardly any laundry got done at all. Even seeing as there was the Prohibition and the law wouldn't allow gin and such, Mama and Nanny never seemed to have any trouble getting it. I'm guessing this was the only way they knew to find some easing from the life of drudgery that'd been handed down to them. I felt real sorry for them.

ON THE FRIDAY NIGHT three days before Christmas some of the neighbors came by to join in the drinking. Mama, Daddy Fletcher, Nanny and the neighbor folks were having a grand time. But not Grandpa.

Grandpa didn't hold with those kinds of goings-on and neither did Mamie. She was disgusted with the rowdiness that filled our little house and had started spending more and more nights out with her teenage friends. Which was fine with me 'cause it meant I had Grandpa all to myself.

Having Grandpa to myself was especially fine since he'd made himself a little apartment in the basement to get away from the drinking. Seemed like things were getting almost back to how they were in Atlanta when I used to follow him to his backyard shed and sit at his knee while he tinkered with his mechanical contraptions. Sometimes he let me take something apart, like a clock, then he'd show me how to put it back together. And he told me about how things work. Trains for instance.

Back in Atlanta sometimes he took me out for a walk to watch the trains. "Looky up yonder how that locomotive pass over," I remember him saying. He was talking about the train trestle that connected the colored part of town with the part where white folks lived. Used to be I'd wonder why the town had to be split up into two different parts like that. Then I decided it was good that at least they were connected.

Grandpa was the only person who made me feel connected like that. Oh Daddy Fletcher's handsome grin still gave me a thrill and I sure was appreciative of the fine piano he bought me. But like Mama he fancied the gin which was worrisome.

Grandpa never worried me. He always gave me the connected feeling. Like when back in Atlanta I used to hold his hand and feel the wind in my face while we watched the train whiz by and listened to the sounds. The spitting steam and the catchy horn tune and the rhythm of the wheels on the tracks all became music in my head. Music that was wrapped up with Grandpa and me and our love of the trains. I always forgot my troubles when I was with Grandpa 'cause he made everything so interesting. And he always answered my questions.

I sat by his knee in his basement apartment while he tinkered with one of his contraptions and a big question popped into my head.

"How do trains work, Grandpa?"

He scrunched his mouth and scratched his head like he always did when he was thinking real hard. "Well, child, it were different inventors that figured how steam could make a locomotive pull a long line of coaches along those tracks. That's 'cause steam be a whole lot more powerful than horses pulling coaches along dirt roads."

"Why's steam so powerful, Grandpa?"

"Steam builds up pressure that makes things move. Things like train locomotives and big ocean ships. Steam engines can move just about anything."

Somehow I knew music had that kind of power too. There's something about the way all the parts of music, like its tune and beat and feelings, come together to make folks feel connected.

That night I dreamed my head was a steam engine. And in this dream I knew the pressure of the music building in my head would make things move someday. Like people's hearts. Like my mama's heart. Sometimes she acted like she got no heart in her body at all. Sometimes she made the Ghost Dog vision rise before me. The vision that always made me feel so scared and alone.

Alone meant being not wanted or loved which I feared more than anything. And there was a reason for me having that fear. The reason was my real daddy. I didn't know who he was and that was scary. It was scary to *me* anyway because it meant I didn't know who *I* was. And neither did Mama. Maybe that's why she didn't love me. And if my real daddy left me why wouldn't Grandpa and Daddy Fletcher leave me too?

6

Messy's Stomp

Saturday morning Grandpa and me were the first ones up. Mamie never came home the night before and everybody else was still laying in bed with bad heads from the gin. I went straight to my piano first thing and started working out some new sounds that had been sizzling inside me.

Grandpa was right cheerful, humming one of his favorite tunes. "I'll pay you fifty cents if you play me that song from my favorite opera," he said.

I looked through my piano rolls. "You mean this one, Grandpa? The Anvil Chorus?"

"That be the one, Messy."

I put in the piano roll and the grandest music I ever heard filled our little parlor. It made my fingers feel like marching. The beats of the music were like hammer blows and Grandpa stomped his foot and clapped his hands right along with those hammer blows, happy as could be.

"Quit the racket!" Nanny yelled from her bedroom. "It giving me the bad head! Can't stand for no racket!"

Grandpa smiled kind of sad and shook his head real slow. "You just carry on with your music, child. If your nanny got the bad head it be her own doing, not yours."

I could hear Nanny moaning in her bed but carried right on like Grandpa said. I put my hands over the keys as they played themselves and let the music's sounds and feelings run though me. When the piano finished doing its magic I played the song myself, just like I'd heard it.

Grandpa smiled and laid a shiny fifty-cent coin on the piano cabinet. "You been blessed with a rare gift, child," he said. "Don't ever let nobody say they's better than you. You got something they'll never have. Something priceless. The way your fingers stomp those keys shows you got more backbone than most anybody I ever knowed, little Messy." He grinned a great big grin which he hardly ever did and patted my shoulder, then disappeared into the shadows of his little basement apartment.

Since it was only two days before Christmas I decided to surprise Grandpa with his very own piano song. I called it "Messy's Stomp." I made the left hand part of the song out of the pounding beat of the Anvil Chorus. The right hand part came from the music leaping around in my head. Sort of a jumpy ragtime tune.

The next day was Christmas Eve and I surprised Grandpa with the new song.

"Why that's might nice of you, Messy," he said in his quiet way.

I figured he didn't like it as much as his favorite opera tunes but he seemed appreciative all the same. I told him I was sorry I hadn't written the song on paper to give him since I didn't know how to read or write music.

"That's all right, Messy," he said. "I'd as soon hear the music come direct from your heart than look at it on a piece of paper. You don't get sounds and feelings from paper."

I thought about what Grandpa said. How the sounds and feelings come direct from your heart. I figured someday I'd learn to read and write the notes on paper. But for now I was happy making music the natural way. I'm guessing there's some value in that too since music that comes more natural most shows what's inside you. Grandpa was right. What comes direct from somebody's heart is real as anything can be.

7

The Johnkankus

Night was falling and was I ever excited even if we didn't have much of a Christmas tree. Daddy Fletcher propped up the scrawny pine tree he'd chopped down near the laboring yard two days before then went to the kitchen to drink gin with Mama.

Nanny said she couldn't stand for no bad head Christmas morning so she was steering clear of the gin. She'd made us a fine supper of the muskie Grandpa caught fresh from the Allegheny River that very day. Now she was helping Mamie and me string popcorn and cut out paper angels to trim our tree.

Some of our neighbors had trees in their houses with

little electric light bulbs that blinked so bright and colorful you'd think they been lit by the Christ child hisself. Grandpa had taken me on a walk down the block after supper and what a sight it was to see all those splendid lights sparkling through the windows.

"I wish we could have pretty lights on our tree," I said while I hung a tinfoil star.

But Nanny said we couldn't afford such nonsense. "That's not what Christmas is about," she said in a way that told me there was no point arguing. "When I was a youngun we didn't worry none about fancy lights. Most exciting thing was how every child rose early Christmas morning to see the Johnkankus."

Mamie rolled her eyes. "You slay me, Nanny," she said, acting all uppity with her teenage slang. "There's no Johnkankus. That's just a crazy legend."

"There be the Johnkankus indeed," Grandpa said.

Nanny looked at him real serious and nodded.

"In olden times the festival of the Johnkankus was the specialest music event for the whole community, both black and white," Grandpa said. "White folks joined in for the music and dancing, but the colored folks knowed the goings-on were really about the ancient African chief Johnkankus."

"Tell me more about the Johnkankus, Grandpa!" I begged, plopping to the floor to listen to his story.

"Come Christmas Eve everybody would dress up in

colorful costumes made from rags and tatters."

"And they wore wild looking masks concocted from all kind of whatnot," Nanny said.

I could tell she was real fired up at the memory.

Mamie sighed and shook her head.

"What about the music?" I asked.

"Oh there was loud songs and chants with lots of rhythm sung to the beat of the gumba boxes," Grandpa said.

"What are gumba boxes, Grandpa?"

"Gumba boxes be nothing but animal skins pulled over a frame, like most any drum. There was other instruments too made from animal bones, sticks, reeds and cow horns. Whatever odds and ends folks could find that would make a joyful noise, like the Good Book say."

I felt like jumping up and down for joy myself. The Johnkankus sounded so exciting. But I stayed put on the floor with my legs crossed, waiting to hear more.

"Was that the main thing folks did at Christmastime? That Johnkankus festival?" I asked.

"Mercy no, child," Nanny said. "Back in slavery days there was always the corn shucking that started the Christmas season."

"Corn shucking?" I said. "What's so festive about that?" It seemed peculiar that such lowdown work could be made into something joyful.

"During the end of November and start of December

the plantation masters invited the slaves of nearby planters to come shuck corn on a particular night," Grandpa said. "And sure enough one or two hundred slaves would sing and shuck corn well-nigh midnight. Then there was a break and the womenfolk served up a fine supper. After about an hour of eatin' the slaves went right on shucking corn till daybreak."

"That sure sounds like a lot of work, Grandpa."

"It surely was, but the music made the work light."

"Tell me about the music!"

"Let's see if I can recollect that Christmas song my pappy used to sing." Grandpa scratched his head and scrunched his mouth. "Oh I remember," he said. "I believe it went like this:

> *Christmas come but once a year*
> *Ho rang du rango*
> *Everyone should have a share*
> *Ho rang du rango.*"

Grandpa slapped his knee to keep time while he sang and Nanny clapped her hands and sang right along. Mama and Daddy Fletcher must've been too far gone with the gin to notice since they stayed put in the kitchen. But I couldn't stay put any longer and jumped to my feet to join in the clapping. Even Mamie couldn't keep from joining in the fine time we were having. She came over and grabbed my hands and we danced a blue streak to Nanny and Grandpa's singing and clapping.

8

Christmas Morning

By the time we finally wore ourselves out with the singing, clapping and dancing I was so tired I don't even know how late I went to bed. But early next morning a good smell woke me. The smell of coffee brewing on the stove. I knew there'd be something good to eat with that coffee too. By and by Nanny would add eggs and corn-meal to the leftover muskie from Christmas Eve supper and fry it up good into croquettes. Fish was always a fine meal, not just for supper but the next morning too.

I tried to lie still a bit longer 'cause I knew Mama and Daddy Fletcher would be in better spirits once they had their coffee. But try as I might I couldn't keep myself in the bed. It was Christmas Day. My mouth watered just thinking about the croquettes and the other delicious smells that would soon be coming from the kitchen. Like deep-fried turkey and juicy yams and collard greens boiled in bacon fat. Smells that seem like they come straight from heaven. And the family all together 'round one table. That was even better than the good smells and delicious tastes.

Grandpa was waiting in the parlor, his cheeks spread in a grin over the surprise he had for me. My stomach did a somersault soon as I saw it. Now I knew what he'd been tinkering with in the basement the Friday night before.

"Looky here, Messy," he said. "A toy train with a real boiler to power the wheels and gears, just like what we seen pass over the trestle back home."

"Thank you kindly, Grandpa! This is the best Christmas present I ever had!"

I don't think I ever saw Grandpa look more pleased. I hugged him hard as I could and his hug back made me feel so loved.

I spent most all day playing with that train except for when we were eating breakfast and dinner. I even made a trestle out of the crate Nanny's Christmas morning eggs came in. I pretended Grandpa and me were back in Atlanta watching the train that connected the colored and white parts of town. And while I listened to the sound of my toy train's boiler I thought about the music inside me busting to get out. The music only Grandpa and me understood about.

THE DAY AFTER CHRISTMAS Nanny sent me down-tairs to hurry Grandpa along. It was Tuesday morning and Daddy Fletcher and him had to get to work at the laboring yard.

"I don't know what's keeping him," Nanny said. "If he's late they'll dock his pay."

I ran down the basement stairs and was surprised to see Grandpa still in bed asleep, peaceful as could be. Not even the faintest snore was coming out of him.

"Grandpa," I said, shaking him real gentle. "You best be getting up. Nanny says you'll be late for work."

He didn't stir.

I shook him harder and spoke a little louder.

"*Grandpa.*"

He lay still as a stone. My belly started to feel tight.

Nanny's voice sailed down from top of the stairs. "What in mercy's name is keeping you two?"

"Grandpa won't wake up," I said in a small voice. I didn't really know why but the inside of my chest felt like a dead weight.

Nanny trudged down the steps, groaning. That was 'cause of her aching bones which always got worse when Grandpa didn't get 'round to things fast enough to suit her.

"I had a might time gettin' down those stairs," she said, breathing real heavy. When she saw how Grandpa lay so still in the bed she bustled over and picked up his wrist. "Mercy on us!" she wailed, dropping his wrist and beating her fist against her big bosom. "*He dead!*"

The floor under my feet seemed to move like there'd been an earthquake. I knew there hadn't been, not really. Only inside me. Tears ran silent down my cheeks and my tight belly felt like it ripped open, leaving nothing but a big dark emptiness.

9

Max

There was a funeral and all kinds of crying and carryings on and neighbor ladies bringing cakes. A lady down the street who came from a place called Italy even brought macaroni and olive oil which was real nice. But it's all blurry to me. A dreadful kind of blurry. Like sinking helpless into a deep black hole.

The shadow of Grandpa's death seemed like there was no end to it and blotted out all the happiness and safe feeling I'd known with him. It terrified me to think how I'd get through the rest of my life without him. And that terror came to life in my visions.

Nighttime was the worst. That time between the sun

going down and falling asleep is when the spooks would come. Like the Ghost Dog with his fearsome red eyes, dripping fangs and white fur sticking out from his monster body. The Ghost Dog and other spooks tormented me through the night. Then I'd stumble to the piano in the morning all fuzzy-eyed.

But the fuzziness started to clear up the minute I laid eyes on Max.

IT WAS NEW YEAR'S EVE which was a Sunday and Nanny said we had relations just come to town.

"They's bereaved like us," she said, wiping the wetness from her eyes with the handkerchief that seemed like it hadn't left her hand since Grandpa died. "Your poor cousin Max. Such a fine boy and his daddy gone to glory in such a terrible way."

"What was the terrible way, Nanny?" I asked.

She shook her head real slow and wiped away another tear. "And that boy's poor, poor mama. I just don't know what's to become of her."

I still wondered about the terrible way but Nanny wasn't in mind to talk about it.

"They's coming for Sunday dinner," Nanny said to Mama.

"They got no business coming here," Mama said. "That Sloane family's bad sorts. When I got the letter about what happened to ol' Max Sloane I think to myself it be just what he deserve."

"Nobody deserve that, 'specially my brother-in-law's son. And I expect this family to be civil to his poor grieving widow and child."

"The way that woman put on airs I got no need to be civil to her. She be nothing but trash if you asks me."

Nanny set her mouth real firm and put her hands on her wide hips. "Young Max and his mama just got here yesterday. Come clear from Savannah to get away from their grief. Feeding them dinner on the Lord's day's the Christian thing to do."

And that was that. Even Mama knew there was no sense arguing. She poured herself a mug of gin.

Nanny started bustling in the kitchen. She cut up a chicken and dipped the parts in cornmeal to fry up on the stove. I'm guessing all the bustling was her way of easing her own grief.

WHEN MAX AND HIS MAMA arrived at our door later that afternoon my knees felt like Nanny's mashed potatoes simmering on the stove. Max was the handsomest boy I'd ever seen. His eyes looked sad but his smile was kind and gentle. The sight of him made things start hopping around inside me like I never felt before.

I didn't say a word during dinner 'cause I knew my tongue would get all tied up with the stuttering. After everybody ate and the grownups were still at the kitchen table talking Max asked if I'd like to go outside with him. I couldn't get out of my seat fast enough. Part of the reason was because the thought of being alone with Max made me shivery excited inside and the other part was I wanted to know what was the terrible way his daddy died.

Max and me put on our coats and went outside to sit on the front stoop. He didn't say anything for the longest time. He set his elbows on his knees and wrung his hands real slow, staring out into the street.

"I'm right sorry about your daddy dying," I said after a spell.

He looked at me and smiled that sweet handsome smile. The smile that did funny things to my insides. Things I didn't understand.

"Well thank you kindly, Mary," he said. "I'm right sorry about your grandpa dying too."

"Thank you kindly, Max."

Max got quiet again and after a time I worked up the guts to ask him. "How'd your daddy die?"

He wrung his hands even harder and sighed real

deep. "He owed money to some men."

"How'd that make him die?"

Max kept staring out at the street and his eyes were shiny wet. "The men he owed money to tied him to the railroad tracks and he got run over by a train."

All my good feelings about trains splintered into a million pieces. Trains were supposed to bring people together, not rip families apart. And for sure they weren't supposed to rip people's bodies apart. Trains were bad as the Ghost Dog. Worse, 'cause a train had killed Max's daddy.

I didn't know what to say so I just stared at him and felt my eyes get wet like his. He looked at me with his sad smile that was also a very brave smile. Then he wrapped both his hands around one of mine and held it tight against his knee. His sadness almost made me forget my own heartache. All I could think was how much I wanted his sadness to go away.

"How old are you, Max?" I finally asked, my voice real quiet.

"Fourteen. And how old are you, Mary?"

"I'm twelve. So I guess you'll be starting up at the high school Tuesday. That'll be my first day in seventh grade at the Lincoln School." I tried to sound cheerful but I don't think my voice came out that way.

"Yeah, I'll be at the high school. I don't know nobody there since my mama and me just got here. What do you say we meet up after school on Tuesday, Mary? I only live a couple blocks from here. Want to take a little walk? I'll show you where."

Did I ever. And he held my hand the whole time.

10

Lincoln School

The day after New Years I walked into the seventh grade classroom at Lincoln School and who do you think was the first person I saw? Amy Frank. She looked prettier than ever with her yellow curls done up in blue silk ribbons that matched her fancy blue dress. I felt real embarrassed about the cheap cotton shift Nanny had stitched together for me the day before. Not to mention the shabby old wool coat that was a hand-me-down from Mamie.

Worst of all were my shoes. Nanny'd decided I had no decent ones so she talked Mama into letting me wear her tiny black Oxfords. Problem was my feet had grown so that half my heels stuck out the back of mama's old shoes. When I hobbled into that classroom I had to abide a lot of sneering looks. Amy's was the worst.

"Don't you got anything better to put on your feet than those beat-down shoes?" she said when I walked past her desk.

I got the burning feeling in my face but kept my eyes down and didn't say a word. Then the teacher came in the room and Amy got real prim and quiet.

"You must be Mary," the teacher said, smiling like she really was glad to meet me.

"Yes, ma'am." I tried hard not to stutter.

"I'm Miss Milholland. Welcome to Lincoln School, Mary."

Miss Milholland was a white lady with silky stockings the same color as her peachy skin and the prettiest legs I ever saw. And her face was like an angel.

"I understand you recently lost your grandfather," she said.

"Yes, ma'am," I said in a low voice, my head hanging.

"Well bless your little heart, sugar," she said, which made me look up with a smile. That felt so good, her calling me sugar. Nobody'd ever called me that before.

That morning I enjoyed looking at Miss Milholland's fine face so much I kept trying to fix my face to look like hers. When the other kids in class noticed me try to hold the different parts of my face in a certain way to look like Miss Milholland some of them pointed and laughed like they thought I was nuts. Miss Milholland shushed them right quick.

Then during music time she couldn't find her little harp to give us the right note to start singing. "Someone must have borrowed it," she said, looking around. "I need a middle C."

I didn't know the names of many notes but I sure enough knew middle C. Mama'd showed it to me on the pump organ, way back when I was little.

I raised my hand. "I can hum the right note, Miss Milholland."

Miss Milholland looked like she didn't believe me. But after she heard the note I hummed she went out in the hall where the piano was and found out I was right.

"Mary has perfect pitch!" she told the class, her eyes wide and amazed. The other kids looked at me like I had horns growing out of my head.

At recess time Miss Milholland hummed a march tune to keep us in line going down the long winding stairs. But before anybody'd gone out the classroom door she stopped humming and looked at me.

"Mary, do you think you could play this march on the piano?"

"I believe so, Miss Milholland." I felt right giddy inside. I went to the piano and played the tune Miss Milholland had hummed and the kids started marching down the stairs in a nice straight line. After a time the march somehow turned into a boogie beat and the kids on the stairs stopped and started acting wild and silly, dancing and holding up the line.

Miss Milholland came over to the piano and gave me a look that said I better go back to playing the march, which I did 'cause I liked Miss Milholland and wanted to please her. But I 'spect she secretly fancied the boogie even if she wouldn't come out and say so. I'm guessing she couldn't 'cause that kind of music wouldn't be fitting at school.

The last kid in line was Amy. She stopped at the piano and smiled at me real sweet. "How'd you learn to play that jazzy music?"

"It comes partly from my visions," I said without thinking.

Her eyebrows got perky. "Visions?"

"Some of my visions are spooks but it's mostly the good visions that help me with my music. I don't know how. They just do."

She kept smiling but her smile started to turn mean. "Well what do you know about that?" she said, then turned to skip down the stairs.

I got my coat and went downstairs to the schoolyard. Amy was a ways off talking to a group of kids. One of the girls pointed at me and snickered and Amy turned to me with her mean smile.

"You filthy darky," she said. "You like to act so weird, but you don't scare us. What business do you have living in this neighborhood or coming to this school anyway? You should've stayed back in Georgia with the other slaves."

"There're no more slaves in Georgia or anyplace else," I said, fuming inside at the idea.

"Well there should be, and you should be one of them 'cause you're just spooky." At that she picked up a stone out of the school yard gravel and threw it at me. It stung my shoulder so I ran at her and shoved her. She grabbed a hunk of my hair and pulled it while other kids joined in, hurling bits of gravel at me and calling me bad names.

I covered my face and started to cry. "Leave me alone!"

"Dry up, you stupid ugly spade!" a boy shouted.

"You nothin' but a witch with your black magic, con-jurin' up ghosts and demons!" yelled another.

"I don't conjure them. The spooks are really there," I said, shaking and tearful.

"You don't know spooks from nothin'!" somebody screeched.

"But I *do* see dreadful visions!" I said, which was probably not very wise.

"Oh, stop beatin' your gums! You're all wet, Scary Mary!" another kid hollered. "We don't believe in your weird visions."

I was so burning mad I wanted to kill all of them. But the bell rang and we had to go back to the classroom.

I don't know what came over me but soon as I saw Miss Milholland's smiling face I grabbed a ruler and swatted her with it, screaming, "You white people made slaves out of us!"

Miss Milholland was upset but she didn't scold me. She just looked very worried and hurt as she rubbed the place on her arm where I hit her. "Oh, you poor child. I wonder who's been telling you such things," was all she said.

I can't tell you how bad I felt. That awful feeling set me to shaking worse than I had in the school yard. I felt terrible about hitting Miss Milholland after she'd been so nice to me that morning.

The shaking got so bad I could hardly stay standing but I ran to the girl's bathroom to hide. My face in the mirror was a sight to behold. I was a blubbering mess. Eyes all scrunched and red and cheeks splotched with tears. Going back to the classroom and facing all those mean kids and Miss Milholland's poor pained face was more than I could stand to think about. I knew she'd never like me anymore. And who could blame her.

The door opened all of a sudden and I jumped and gulped. It was Miss Milholland. I could see her sweet pretty face in the mirror and I wanted to curl up and die.

Her smile was kind but her eyes were worried. "Tell me what's wrong, Mary," she said.

I stared down into the wash basin. I wanted to tell her how bad I felt about hitting her. But the words were trapped inside my bone-dry throat.

Miss Milholland just stood there, her smile so very gentle.

"I been cursed," I said finally, my voice so quiet I hardly could hear myself.

"Cursed? What do you mean?"

"I been cursed since the day I was born. My mama told me so."

Miss Milholland moved closer to me till I could feel her breath on the back of my neck. Then I felt her hand on my shoulder. "Mary, what exactly did your mother tell you?" The sweetness of her voice made me want to cry worse than if she'd bawled me out.

"My mama says I'm cursed 'cause I was born with the sign of the caul," I said, spilling over with shame.

Miss Milholland's hand that had been resting on my shoulder fell to her side. She folded her arms. "The caul? Why that's nothing but a membrane that protects a baby inside its mother. Sometimes the caul's still sticking to a newborn baby. It's perfectly natural. You're not cursed, Mary."

I looked up into the mirror and saw her smile like she

knew exactly what she was talking about. I turned around, blinking hard as I could to clear the tears from my eyes.

"In fact," she went on, her eyes and smile bright, "I understand that in medieval times it was believed a baby born with their caul was destined for greatness."

"Medieval times? When was that?" I asked, sniffling and wiping my eyes with my fists.

"Hundreds of years ago, before people knew very much about science or medicine." She paused a minute and looked more serious. "I have a feeling about you, Mary. I do believe you're destined for greatness, and not because of the caul. Your musical ability is outstanding, and I know you're going to do great things with that."

"Do you really think so, Miss Milholland?" For the first time in a very long time I felt a tiny spark of hope.

"I certainly do. God has given you a remarkable gift, and it's your duty to share that gift with others."

I didn't know what to say. All I could think was Miss Milholland was the wisest, kindest person in the world and I was the dumbest and meanest because I'd hit her for no reason.

THAT DAY WAS SO AWFUL. About as bad as a day could ever be. Even after Miss Milholland's kindness and saying I was destined for greatness. For the rest of the afternoon I sat in misery and waited and waited for the big old school bell to ring. I remembered what Max said about us meeting up after school and all I could think about was seeing him again.

By the time the bell finally rang I was so wore out with the waiting I hardly had strength to move. But once I was outside I ran fast as my feet could carry me to Max's house. He wasn't there and neither was his mama so I sat on the front step whimpering.

A while later he came gliding down the street on his shiny blue bicycle, his book bag hanging on his shoulder. My heart danced at the sight of him. I jumped to my feet and when he saw me he skidded to a stop. The tires made a crunchy sound on the street gravel and blew up a little cloud of dust.

"Mary!" he said, and a big handsome smile lit up his face. He walked his bike across the sidewalk and leaned it against the railing by the steps. He sloped his shoulder and shook it to let the book bag slide off, which he caught with his other hand and hung on the railing post. My heart went to pieces at the sight of his fine strong shoulders. I wanted to hug him and press into him like I used to with Grandpa.

He scrunched his forehead. "What's wrong with you, Mary? You look like you seen a ghost or something."

I started bawling right there on the sidewalk and Max came over and put his arms around me in a strong but gentle way like Grandpa used to do. I buried my face in his shoulder and the story of my awful day came pouring out.

"Well dang those white kids," he said. "They got no business talking to anybody like that, 'specially a sweet nice girl like you, Mary."

His kind words made me cry even more. I squeezed his shirt with my fists.

"I feel awful about poor Miss Milholland. She's so nice, saying encouraging things to me. And I had to go and hit her. For no reason at all except I was so mad at those bullies on the playground."

"Sounds like your teacher understands about all that. She's not gonna hold nothing against you and don't you worry your head about it for another minute, you hear?"

I nodded against his shoulder and my insides got bouncy and tingly. It was a strange but wonderful feeling. Love I guess. If this was love then love sure does peculiar things to your body parts. Good things.

Max tightened his arms around me and spoke in a real gentle way. "You just keep at your music, Mary, and won't nobody bother you no more."

I backed away a little and looked up at him. "How'd

you know about my music, Max?'

He grinned kind of sheepish. "Well, I came over to see you yesterday and when I got there I heard this beautiful piano music coming through your parlor window. When I peeked inside and saw you playing I couldn't hardly believe it. I just stood there for the longest time and listened. I didn't want to bother you none 'cause you looked like you were concentrating so hard. Almost like you were in another world."

I was too filled up with happiness to speak. Max understood about my music like Grandpa had. Now I was sure the strange feelings in my body parts meant I was in love.

11

Beethoven

All I could think about was Max. He knew just what to say and how to hold me to make me feel better. And he understood about my music like nobody else in my family ever did except Grandpa. I wanted to be with Max forever.

There were so many things that could go wrong though. Like his mama. And my mama. They didn't take to each other and might try to keep Max and me apart. I found out why by listening in on the grownups talking late that night after Max and his mama came for dinner, when I was supposed to be in bed. Seemed Max's mama didn't hold with my mama's gin drinking and my mama thought Max's mama put on airs, like she'd said to Nanny. Well it didn't matter how our mamas got on. Max and me got on just fine.

But an awful feeling told me we wouldn't always be together which set my body to shaking. Without Max that big hole in me he was starting to fill would be empty again and I was afraid then I'd shrivel up and there'd be nothing left to feed my music. Even if my music had gotten me into trouble with the kids at school, I still feared losing it.

I didn't know what I feared more. Losing Max or losing my music.

FOR THE WHOLE REST OF THAT FIRST WEEK at school Miss Milholland brought me presents every day. Little things mostly like movie magazines and chewing gum which she gave me when nobody was looking. The best present of all was a book about the famous composer Beethoven. It was an old book, one the school librarian didn't want anymore.

Nobody'd ever given me my very own book before. I was so excited my hands shook when Miss Milholland handed it to me. On the front was a picture of Beethoven with wild looking hair and eyes that looked like they were fixing to slay a dragon. I could hardly wait to get home and read all about him.

That night I read the book cover to cover. Beethoven's sad life brought tears to my eyes. His cruel father, the way people thought he was peculiar because he looked funny, and most of all his deafness which he said drove him near to despair. *I would have ended my life. It was only my art that held me back. Ah, it seemed to me impossible to leave the world until I had brought forth all that I felt was within me.*

Tears streamed down my cheeks as I read those words Beethoven had written in a letter to his brothers. I knew how he felt. And for some reason the stories Grandpa told me about the slaves suddenly flooded my mind. Slavery was like a prison. And Beethoven was alive during the time of slavery. Only he was trapped in the prison of his own deafness. A prison he knew he couldn't ever escape from. He must have shared the slaves' hopeless feelings. And their suffering.

12

The Steam Iron

Saturday morning after my first week at Lincoln School Nanny was waiting for me in the kitchen. I'd just woke up and my head was filled with dreams of Max.

"You best not be making doe eyes over that boy," Nanny said, "or sure as sure be a whippin' later." Her mouth was set in one flat line. "You know your mama don't hold with that family."

How'd she know what I was thinking about? Nanny must have the second sight too, I thought.

"But Max is so nice," I told her.

"His mama's flighty as a June bug and you best believe whatever's on that boy's mind can't be good. Takes after his daddy, he do."

"His mama might be flighty, Nanny, but he's real kind and so smart."

"That's what he'd have you believe, now ain't it?" Nanny's lips got even tighter and she put her hands on her broad hips. Her disapproving look.

"I thought you liked Max and his mama, Nanny."

"I felt sorry for them, is all. But it come to me that your mama's right. Max's daddy was a bad sort and no telling what be on that boy's mind. And his mama puts on airs, just like your mama say."

I thought about the whippin' she said I'd sure as sure get and decided not to argue with Nanny. She'd sure as sure tell Mama and I was in no mind for a sore backside. I thought I best keep quiet.

Nanny folded her arms across her big bosom and kept looking at me with the cross look. "Girl, I don't know what's to become of you, your head in the clouds day and night. Sometimes I don't think you got the sense the Good Lord give a pigeon."

"My head's not in the clouds, Nanny. You know how hard I work at my music."

"Yeah, I knows it. Don't I have to listen to that racket till my head feel like it gonna pop?"

Nanny calling my music racket hurt my feelings. But I tried not to show it. I lifted my chin a little. "Miss Milholland likes my music. She asks me to play the piano in the hall every day while the kids march down the stairs to recess."

"Hmmph. That teacher got no taste if you asks me."

"I wish you didn't feel that way, Nanny."

"Don't matter what I feel. Like I said, it just ain't practical. What you gonna do when the day come you gots to fend for yourself?"

"I'll fend for myself playing piano. Miss Milholland says I'm destined for greatness with my music."

Nanny shook her head. "You just like your mama. Never a day in her life that girl's had a sensible head on her shoulders. Since the day she was born her head's been clouded up, first with the music, now with the drink."

And you with the drink too, Nanny, I thought but didn't say.

The last thing I wanted was to be like her. Or like Mama. That thought scared me more than most anything. I was afraid if I kept listening to Nanny I'd have one of my terrible visions, the ones that always came when I was scared.

But Nanny paid my fears no mind. She just stood there with her arms folded, glaring at me. "I aim to teach you how to press and fold the white folks's linens so's they keep that crisp look," she said.

"But I'm scared of the steam iron, Nanny."

"Scared my eye. It's time you got your head out of the

clouds and learn something useful. When you're poor you gots to grow up fast."

And that was that.

I wanted to help. I really did. But I couldn't forget the time back in Atlanta when I was only about five and I tried to help Mama. It was a Friday afternoon and the drinking had already started. I noticed there was some ironing left undone. The wood stove's still crackling, I thought. I'll heat up the flatiron and finish Mama's work for her. When the iron started steaming I picked it up and was it ever heavy. Well wouldn't you know it just slipped from my little fist and landed on my other arm before it went clattering to the floor. I howled from the pain and Mama came running. When she saw what I'd done she grabbed a wooden spoon and swatted the backs of my legs which of course only made me howl all the more.

Grandpa spread chicken grease on my burnt arm then distracted me from my bawling by setting me on his knee and telling a story I never forgot.

13

The Good Spirit

While I helped Nanny press and fold the white folks' linens my head got filled with Grandpa and the story he'd told me that day I got burned. I remembered sitting on his knee and cuddling against him and feeling comforted by his warmth and the beat of his heart while he talked about the slave days.

"My pappy tell me how when he was a little'un he lived with his kind old grandma in a old wood hut," Grandpa'd said. "Then one day he learned the sorry fact that not only the hut but his grandma herself belonged to a mysterious person called Old Massa. It was then that clouds and shadows began to hover all around him, because this Old Massa's name was only mentioned with fear and shuddering. Later my pappy was to learn the even sorrier fact that he'd soon be taken away from his grandma to work for Old Massa."

"What kind of work this Old Massa make your pappy do, Grandpa?" I asked.

"Come cotton season he worked in the field with the other slaves, picking cotton all day till his fingers bled."

"That's so sad," I said, sniffling in my five-year-old way.

"Yes, child, it were sad indeed. My pappy always remembered the happy days when he was little, though, the days before he knowed he was a slave."

"Was he always sad after that?"

"Well, like the other darkies he got a bit of easing from his sadness when the Good Spirit come."

"Was the Good Spirit Jesus, Grandpa?"

"Some say it was. Others say it was the shared spirit of their African ancestors, come to ease the burden of slavery. Nobody really knows. Only one thing's for sure. The Good Spirit come as music that reached deep inside the slaves, turning their anguish into joy."

Calling to mind Grandpa's story reminded me of my own life. I wasn't a slave but I felt haunted by the same clouds and shadows. The visions that came to me at night or even during the day when I least expected them. I figure my visions must have been a help to me in that way because whenever I played my music a spirit would come and I'd close my eyes and go away somewhere. Like Max said, I'd go to another world.

The memory of Grandpa's story brought me to mind of how the slaves figured a way to get their feelings across with music by singing spirituals and work songs. I knew the spirit that came to me must be the same one that came to the slaves and turned their anguish into joy.

The Good Spirit Grandpa told of became more and more important to me. A kind of religion. Something that filled my heart and fed my soul. I needed that because something very important was missing from my life. That's 'cause after we moved north my mama didn't play organ for church anymore. Truth was we fell away from going to church altogether. I missed it. Not just 'cause of the organ but because of the Good Spirit feeling I always got there. The only other way I ever got that Good Spirit feeling was with my music.

14

The Church Organ

After I helped Nanny with the ironing that Saturday morning I snuck out of the house to do some exploring. Before long I came to a lovely street called Highland Avenue. The loveliness of the street wasn't what I noticed most though. What filled my eyes was the biggest, tallest, most awesome looking church I ever saw.

I bent my head back far as I could to try and see to the top. It was a smoggy day as usual so I couldn't even see the highest part. But it seemed some of the pointy parts on top went so high they must've reached up to heaven. To the Almighty hisself. All I could think was the angels must be hovering up there over this heavenly place. That was 'cause of how the little rays of sun peeked through the smoky sky and shown all around the church steeple and seemed to hug it and bounce off it then hug it again. There must be something alive up there, I thought. Something wonderful.

I walked over and looked at the sign in front. East Liberty Presbyterian Church. I didn't know what Presbyterian meant. I couldn't even say the word. All I knew was whoever built this church sure knew how to make something that could amaze folks and bring them together. Who wouldn't want to come to a beautiful place like this?

Oh I knew I shouldn't but I decided to peek inside. What a sight. I felt like I'd walked into the Lord's kingdom. And there was music. Organ music. I somehow knew this even though it didn't sound a thing like the little pump organ back at the storefront church in Atlanta. This organ music sounded like it come straight from God. How my fingers ached to play that glorious organ.

Then something peculiar happened. I felt a vision coming and before I knew it I was part of the vision. I was three years old and back in the little storefront church with my mama. She was practicing on the pump organ and I was running around like a wild thing.

"Mary, what you up to? Come over here and sit still

so's you can't get into no trouble," Mama said. "Come over here directly, Little Miss Mary, before I whup you good!"

I scurried over and climbed onto Mama's lap. She went on with her practicing with me right there on her knee and I listened with fascination. And as I watched her fingers move I somehow always knew what note she was getting ready to play.

When she finished and was fixing to play another hymn wouldn't you know my little hands beat hers to the keyboard and I picked out a melody. She dropped me then and there and I started to bawl.

Mama paid no mind to my wailing. She ran out the front door. I bawled all the louder but a couple minutes later she came back with some of the neighbor ladies. "Stop your hollering, Mary!" she yelled. "Show these ladies what you just did."

I sniffled and rubbed my eyes with my tiny fists then reached for the organ keys. Somehow my little fingers knew just what to do. I played my favorite church song:

What a friend we have in Jesus,
all our sins and griefs to bear!
What a privilege to carry
everything to God in prayer!

While I played I felt a great big smile spread across my face.

The neighbor ladies about went to pieces. They started talking all at once.

"Sweet Jesus!"

"Good Lord in heaven!"

"This child been blessed by the angels above!"

Their praise gave me such a warm feeling. Mama just stared at me with the hard look.

"It be the birth sign of the caul that give that aptness," she said after the ladies left. "Ain't nobody ever see a three-year-old child play organ like that before. I reckon you be even stranger than I thought. I reckon you be cursed."

I got the shaking crying feeling, the kind a three-year-old gets. But I wasn't three. I was twelve and standing alone in the big old Presbyterian church in East Liberty. The vision I'd just had was real, though. It was something that happened almost ten years before. Something I'd forgotten about. But now I remembered and the memory left me with very mixed up feelings.

15

Georgia Skin

"Where's Daddy Fletcher?" I asked Nanny when I got home from the church. He and Mama'd been sleeping all morning but I figured he'd be up by now. I wanted to talk to him about my mixed up feelings. The caul, my visions and my music were muddled together in my head which told me somehow those things were all connected. But I couldn't figure how. Daddy Fletcher would know. He always made things seem so straightened out.

"Your stepdaddy be in the kitchen smiling, all pleased at hisself," Nanny said, her mouth tight and disapproving.

She seemed to be moving slower these days. The washing and ironing always made her bones ache but she said since Grandpa passed she got the aching deep in her bones worse than ever. I knew Nanny meant this. She missed Grandpa much as I did. Maybe more.

But I knew another reason why Nanny's mouth was tight. It was because even though Daddy Fletcher worked hard every day carrying cement blocks at the laboring yard, come nighfall he'd trade his laborer's overalls for the fine suit and vest he wore when he went to his real business which was gambling. I found this out soon after Mama and him got married. I also knew that was how he got the money to buy me my piano.

I went in the kitchen and Daddy Fletcher was sitting at the table with a big grin on his face, counting money. He always came home happy when he won at cards. And from the look of the money pile on the kitchen table he must've won big the night before.

I never got to ask him about my mixed up feelings because he started talking about his gambling ventures. "I'm in mind to take you with me over to Frankstown Avenue tonight, Baby Doll," he said. "To bring me luck."

"Frankstown Avenue? Where's that, Daddy Fletcher?"

"It's East Liberty's most famous street 'cause that's where all the night clubs, theaters and gambling joints are."

I felt my eyes grow big. "Am I allowed to go to those kinds of places?"

"The card players will all be men 'cause women aren't allowed at gambling joints. But I just bought myself a extra large coat to put you under and sneak you in."

Sure enough that very night Daddy Fletcher snuck me into his gambling joint hidden under his big scratchy overcoat. There was a dusty old piano against one wall and the place was filled with cigarette smoke and men in zoot suits playing cards. The men looked up when we came in then went back to their card playing. They looked like gangsters which I thought was exciting. I watched their card game with fascination.

"That game's called Georgia Skin, Baby Doll," Daddy Fletcher told me. Then he put his hat on the gambling table and threw in a dollar. "I want everybody to put some money in this hat for my little girl to play piano for you."

The Georgia Skin game came to a stop and the dollars started rolling in. I sat at the piano and played and played till my fingers near gave out.

Out on the sidewalk after we finally left Daddy Fletcher took the money out of his hat and counted it. He whistled. "Thirty dollars! And all 'cause of you beatin' out a few tunes on that rickety piano. Now what you got to say about that, Baby Doll?"

"I say let's do this often as we can." Maybe this was

what Miss Milholland meant by sharing my gift of music with others.

Daddy Fletcher put the money back in his hat and grinned. "Best we do this every Saturday night, don't you say?" He winked and held out his hat to me. "Now give me back the dollar I put in here to start your tips, Baby Doll."

I gladly reached in the hat and handed Daddy Fletcher back his dollar which he stuffed in his pocket. Then he popped me a Pez, the peppermint candy everybody'd been hankering for lately. What a treat. My mouth was full of minty juice from the Pez but I smiled up at Daddy Fletcher to show him my thanks. He smiled back and wrapped his big strong hand around my little one and we walked home together, the hat full of dollars safe under his other arm. We didn't tell Mama about the money or where we'd been.

I loved that little secret between Daddy Fletcher and me. It was our special mystery. A kind of veil, like the veil I was born with. I was starting to make some sense out of my mixed up feelings. The caul had a purpose more than just the ghosts and visions that had spooked me for so long. Like Miss Milholland said, maybe it meant I was destined for great things with music. And sure enough getting thirty dollars in tips was a great thing.

16

The Blues

I thought Nanny would have the cross look Sunday morning because of me going to the gambling joint with Daddy Fletcher. But she was in the kitchen humming her favorite song, "My Mama Pinned a Rose on Me." I'd heard Nanny sing that song my whole life and knew all the words by heart:

> *My mama pinned a rose on me,*
> *She pinned it where everybody could see,*
> *Everybody's talking 'bout the way I do.*
> *I'm gonna leave this hard-luck town,*
> *I'm gonna leave before the sun goes down,*
> *Everybody's talking 'bout the way I do.*

I went to the piano and played the song and while I played I sang the words. I thought this would please Nanny. It didn't.

"What's that caterwaulin' I hear?" she shouted from the kitchen. "You can't carry a tune with both hands, girl!"

Nanny was right. My hands were meant for making music at the piano, not my voice for singing. I didn't try to sing the words again but the sweetness of the song's tune made me smile and get prickly-eyed at the same time. I thought about the rose in that song, about its beauty and goodness and that gave me a wonderful feeling.

Not that the feeling the song gave me had anything to do with my mama. It had to do with Daddy Fletcher. I knew from how proud he was of me at the gambling joint the night before that he prized my ability as a piano player. And he'd told those gambling men I was his very own little girl. Like I was worth something.

"Play some blues for me, Baby Doll," Daddy Fletcher said from across the room and my heart near jumped right out of me. I hadn't heard him come in the parlor.

"Blues? What's that, Daddy Fletcher?" I said, my heart a-leaping and hopping with happiness at all the special attention he was giving me.

"The blues come from slavery," he said, "from spiri-tuals and field hollers, and from the chants of our

African ancestors."

"What do blues sound like?" I asked.

"Let me whistle you some." Daddy Fletcher puckered his lips and whistled about the saddest, sweetest tune I ever heard.

"Hear those sad notes, Baby Doll?" he said when he'd finished. "Those are blue notes. Woes and tribulations are in those notes."

He went on with his whistling and I listened careful as I could. Then I tried to play what I heard on the piano, crushing and sliding those blue notes with the fire that came straight from my heart.

For the rest of that day I thought about what Daddy Fletcher said. How the blues come from slavery. It brought to mind the story Grandpa told me about the Good Spirit being the shared spirit of the slaves' African ancestors. And I realized something. Now that there was no more slavery and no new spirituals or field hollers the Good Spirit was moving through a new kind of music—the blues.

Daddy Fletcher was so moved by my blues playing he paid me fifteen dollars. Part of the money he'd won at the gambling joint the night before. Fifteen dollars was only half what I earned playing piano there but still a fortune. I hid that money from Mama so she couldn't take it from me. I'd gladly give it over if it wasn't for the fact she'd just use it to buy booze. So I stuffed the money under my mattress.

In a way I felt bad about this but I knew I didn't have a choice. I couldn't abide the notion of the money I earned being thrown away on gin. It turned my stomach to think about it. Mama's gin drinking was a wicked thing and I sure as the devil's fire didn't want any part of it.

Which brought to mind something else about Mama that wearied me right down to my bones. How she didn't know or even care who my real daddy was. You'd think I would have stopped fretting about this now that Daddy Fletcher'd come into our lives. But I was still troubled. What troubled me most was how Mama'd always tacked a name to the end of mine. The name of a man called Scruggs who she knew before I was born. That's what she'd always told everybody my name was, Mary Scruggs. I hated that name.

So when Mama married Daddy Fletcher I decided it was okay to make my name like his. I figured someday I might have to change it legal or at a church or something. But I hoped the law wouldn't notice and folks in the neighborhood and teachers at my new school would think I came by the name natural. That I was Daddy Fletcher's true and rightful little girl.

17

Grandpa's Basement

After I stuffed the fifteen dollars Daddy Fletcher gave me under my mattress I went back to my piano to practice more. Out the parlor window who should I see but Max gliding down the street with no hands, swaying his body just a little to keep his bicycle in line. The sight of him made me quivery inside. A good quivering, not the kind I got from dreams and visions of the Ghost Dog. I rushed out the front door.

"Helloooooo, Mary!" he called to me in his cheery way, his handsome face all lit up with a grin.

"Max!" I yelled, running toward him. I wished I had a bicycle so I could fly down the street free as a bird like

Max. But I didn't even know how to ride one anyway.

There *was* something I could do that Max couldn't, though. "Wanna hear the new song I been working on?" I asked him.

"Sure!" He skidded his bicycle to a stop and jumped off handy as a blue jay landing in its nest after an easy flight through the sky.

My leaping heart about jumped out of me. "Come on inside then," I said, trying not to sound too excited. I didn't want him to know how shivery I felt.

He followed me into the house and over to the piano. I sat down and started playing my latest rendition of "My Mama Pinned a Rose on Me." That song had come to be my specialty. I'd dressed it up so much with all the bluesy jittery sounds I'd been working on it hardly sounded anymore like the simple little tune Nanny always sang.

When I finally finished Max looked like his eyes were about to pop out of his head. "Lord Almighty, Mary, where in blazes you learn to play like that? I heard you play before, but never like that!"

"Nobody ever really taught me," I said. "I just like to sit at the piano getting my own sounds. If I let my fingers dance around long enough they always come up with something."

"That *something* is like nothing I ever heard. You should be playing piano at one of those swank night clubs. That's where you belong if you ask me."

I was so pleased by Max's praising words my cheeks went hot. "I'll play some more if you like," I said kinda shy-like. I didn't want Max to get wore out from my music. What if he decided it was devil music like Nanny said? My leaping heart would sink right back into a deep hole if he thought that.

Turned out Max couldn't get enough of my piano playing. And whenever he was by my side my heart leaped around so much that music bounced in my head like a bunch of India rubber balls. But I needed time to work things out. Alone time which was hard to get at my house. And between Daddy Fletcher whistling me the blues and Max making my heart jump like a leap frog, notes had been popping up in my head faster than I could think. My fingers couldn't keep up. So I pounded the music out on the piano one part at a time then tried to put it all together real slow.

Sometimes I had to do that pounding of each part over and over. I told myself that was okay because I'd read in the book Miss Milholland gave me that Beethoven put his music together in the same way. Or right near the same way. He had a music idea then hummed or banged it on the piano over and over till that idea mixed with other ideas. And somehow after a long time of working it all out it came together into a glorious piece of music. That's the way it worked with me too. So

I figured if my way of making music was like Beethoven's then my way must be just fine.

I wondered if Beethoven was born with the caul like me. But the book didn't say anything about that. I figured he must have been though 'cause it sure seemed like he was destined for greatness no matter what. His way of making music came from his suffering and the best music comes from suffering like Grandpa said. The Good Spirit makes that happen. So the Good Spirit must've come to Beethoven like it did to the black slaves at that time. Like it came to me.

But caul or no caul, Good Spirit or no Good Spirit, with all the commotion in my house it was hard to find a way to make sense of the music that was swirling in my head. I decided I needed my own separate space. Someplace I'd feel safe where nobody could hurt or shame me. Where could that be? I wondered. It was a problem in a small house with five family members and people coming and going all the time.

So I took to sleeping in the basement where Grandpa used to spend his time. It was the most peaceful place in the house. A place where I could think and dream and get some sleep.

My relations paid no mind to me staying in the basement. Truth be told I think they were pleased about my decision to keep to myself. It suited them fine and it suited me too 'cause sometimes in the basement I felt

Grandpa's spirit there with me which was comforting. I smelled his familiar scent. His workman smell that was like laundry starch, motor oil and fresh-cut woodchips all mixed together. That smell always made me so happy. I ached for that smell same as I ached for Grandpa's wise words and comforting touch.

The tears that burned and soaked my eyes whenever I thought about Grandpa helped save me from staying torn up inside. That torn up feeling would come right out through my eyes at night when I lay on Grandpa's little cot, missing him so bad. And whatever torn pieces were left would work their way through my fingers the next morning when I went to my piano.

18

Teacher Ladies

Miss Milholland must've told the other teacher ladies at Lincoln School about my musical know-how 'cause they started having me come to their boardinghouse to play for them. They even gave me Kool-Aid which let me tell you was a real treat. My favorite flavor was root beer. And when they saw I was hungry they gave me a wonderful snack I'd never tasted before. A peanut butter and jelly sandwich. If anything'll coat your stomach and keep the hunger pangs from taking hold that sure will. Not quite a match for a fine meal of ham hocks and yams and collard greens but it'll sure do in a pinch when your belly's twisting and growling.

Before long I was going to the teachers' boarding-house every day after school and playing up a storm. They were so pleased and happy with what I played they gave me dimes and quarters and sometimes even dollar bills. Then I went home with all that money tied up in my handkerchief.

I didn't tell Mama the teacher ladies were paying me to play piano for them 'cause I knew she'd take the money from me. Instead I saved until I had enough to go to the second-hand store down the street and buy myself a pretty dress and nice shoes that fit. When Mama asked how I came to be dressed so fancy I lied and told her my teacher gave me these things to wear when I went to the boardinghouse.

Mama seemed content with this answer but Nanny soon grew suspicious. One day I came home skipping with gladness, all dolled up in my special dress and shoes, to find Nanny standing on the front step glaring at me. Her lips were pinched tight and her hands were on her broad hips.

"Look at you struttin' round fancy as you please. What wickedness you been up to, child, running around East Liberty like some kinda heathen? Proud as a peacock you is, playing that evil music."

"It's not evil music, Nanny, it's jazz. That's the new music everybody hankers for now. Even the teacher ladies."

"Jazz my foot. You can call that clamor what you want, but it's from the devil is all I know. And it ain't proper."

"Why do you say that, Nanny? The teacher ladies like my music. It makes them happy."

"The devil don't attract folks by making 'em sad, now does he? That music you call jazz brings a false happiness that leads right down the road to Satan's fiery furnace."

I smiled humble-like. "Sorry, Nanny."

I didn't mention that she and Mama were paving a faster road to that fiery furnace with their gin drinking. It wouldn't be fitting to talk that way to older folks. Old folks are owed respect even if they do act ornery at times. So I kept quiet. But the Ghost Dog came to visit me that night. Next morning I tried to talk to Nanny about it.

"Mary, stop asking so many questions," she scolded. "Why you have to be different from reg'lar folks, carrying on like a conjure man with your spooks and visions?"

I wasn't carrying on. I'd only asked to know more about the Ghost Dog. About why he chased that boy Nanny told me about. But she was tired of telling me that story. She didn't understand that the Ghost Dog still haunted me which was why I wanted to know more about it. But Nanny didn't like a lot of questions. I couldn't figure how else to find things out, so I kept asking.

"Please tell me more about that Ghost Dog," I pestered, even though Nanny had the cross look on her face.

"What'd I tell you, missy?" she snapped back at me. "I'm weary of you always asking about that confounded dog. Now leave me be."

Even Nanny was tired of my visions. I'd have to figure out the Ghost Dog's reason for haunting me on my own.

19

Music and Max

Soon as I got home from school the next day I saw Max riding his bike towards my house. My heart danced with joy. I looked at his hands clutching the handlebars and closed my eyes and pretended it was me he was holding. Sure enough once he skidded his bike to a stop he looked at me with his handsome grin and put his arms around me in a protecting way, like Grandpa used to do.

My insides went a-hopping and the hopping felt good. Max gave me such a fine feeling inside. All warm and safe. I wanted more than anything to hold onto that feeling and never let go. Only thing was those good feelings were making me think more and more about

Max and less and less about my music.

Best of all was music and Max. But it seemed like Max was bringing me a lot more love than my music was 'specially after how Nanny carried on about my music being from the devil. Something deep inside told me I best not forget about my music, though, even if when Max was around I just couldn't help it.

I decided to fess up to Max about the Ghost Dog.

"Where'd you ever hear about such a thing?" he asked.

"My nanny told me how it would rise up out of the Georgia swamp. I seen it myself, not only in the swamp down south but here in East Liberty. I just seen it last night hovering over my bed."

"Your nanny's from the old times, Mary, all filled up with ghosts and the devil and such. Pay her no mind."

"You sound like Grandpa," I said, with a sad feeling.

"Sounds like your grandpa had some sense in his head. You should've listened to him."

I guess I should've," I said, hanging my head.

Max lifted my chin ever so gentle and touched his lips to mine. The warmest most tingly feeling I ever felt went all through me. "Well I got to get home now," he said.

But the next day after school he came back to listen some more to my music. I was feeling down and started to play for him in a kind of lopy way. But soon the music in my head and the excitement of having Max at my side got me going. The blood started rushing through my hands making them leap around something fierce.

"How do you do that?" he asked when I was finished. His eyes were wide with amazement like they always were when I played for him.

I shrugged my shoulders and tried to sound casual. "I just enjoy myself. The piano's a natural place for me to be. I don't know what's going to come of it."

"I think great things will come of it, just you wait and see, Mary." His eyes were so kind and his smile so handsome I felt like melting butter.

He scrunched his eyes like Grandpa used to do. "How do you move your fingers like that?"

"I practice with my mind and my mind moves my fingers. I don't worry about my hands at all. Just my mind."

"But . . . I don't see how a *girl* can play like that."

"I don't think much about being a girl when I play piano," I told him. "If you get carried away in your work you really don't know if you're a girl or a boy."

"Well *I* know you're a girl," he said, grinning.

My heart went wild with fluttering but I tried to act easygoing. "I never worry myself about looking like a girl when I play. You can't be worrying about looking good. When you're playing piano you just have to lose yourself in the music."

"You may play like a man, but you're a girl all right, and a very pretty one too." His grin brightened and his eyes sparkled.

In my excitement I leaped from the piano bench to hug him. But suddenly I felt shy and lowered my eyelashes. "Nobody else thinks I'm much to look at," I said.

"Pay no mind to what they say, Mary. To me you're the most beautiful girl in the world," he said in a voice so kind and sweet my knees turned to jelly.

Then he put his arms around me and kissed me ever so warm and gentle on the lips. My fluttering heart about jumped out of my chest. He smiled at me and winked then told me he had to go. His mama was expecting him.

I liked it that Max paid his mama so much mind. That was a fine thing for a boy to do and meant he knew how to treat ladies nice.

20

The Tea Party

Miss Milholland and the other teacher ladies must've really liked the jazzy music I played at their boarding-house 'cause they planned a tea party in my honor. All the girls in my class were invited and their mothers too.

I told Mama about the tea party and she seemed right pleased. She even got up early the morning of the party and fixed my hair in a bouncy ponytail like the white girls. Well not exactly like the white girls' pony-tails. Mama put some stuff in my hair that softened its wiriness and made it fall out of the ribbon that tied it back in pretty little coils. What a fine time that was with Mama. She hardly ever spent nice time with me like that.

Even if my hair didn't look quite like white girls' hair the new style made me feel prettier than I'd ever looked. So did the new flowered dress I'd bought with my tips from the gambling joint and been saving for such an occasion. Guess I fibbed a little to Max when I told him I never thought about looking like a girl. Truth be told I was so excited about my special party I hardly could stand the tingling going through my body. Best of all was how Mama was finally so proud of me.

I wore my flowered dress to school that day so I'd be ready for the tea party which was to take place at the teacher ladies' boardinghouse right after school. The tingling that started early that morning never let up and did that day ever seem long. All I could think about was Mama sitting there in the teacher ladies' parlor with the other mothers smiling and oh so pleased with me.

When I finally heard the clang of the giant old school bell at three o'clock I couldn't get out the door fast enough. Miss Milholland and the other teachers let me walk with them to the boardinghouse and I pranced along beside them feeling like I'd bust from happiness.

It was only a short walk and soon after we got to their house the other girls and their mamas started coming. I hoped the mamas would make a fuss over my hair and my dress and how pretty I looked. But not the kind of fuss that really means *Well aren't you pret-ty—for a colored girl.* I wanted them to think I was pretty like their little girls. I sat in a straight-backed wooden chair with my ankles crossed and my hands folded in my lap waiting. I was fixing to play some of my newest music for all the guests. Then we'd have tea and cake.

I waited and waited for Mama to come. It got to be three-thirty then four and the big clock on the sideboard kept ticking. The mothers sat around smiling kind of stiff and saying things like, "Well, isn't this just lovely?" I was feeling less and less lovely as the minutes ticked by and no Mama. After a while my heart started to sink like there was no bottom to it. No place for it to be caught and stop sinking and be safe. It just kept sink-ing. And Mama never came.

21

Scary Mary

It's funny the kinds of things that make you cry. The one nice thing about the teacher ladies' party was the way Mama had fixed my hair. Oh I'd played the piano good enough and the teachers and girls and their mamas clapped and smiled so polite. One of the mothers said, "That was so fine, dear. You keep up the good work, you hear?"

Her smile was so pretty. She made me feel like I belonged. Like I was one of the white girls. It wasn't quite the same feeling I'd have if my own mama came and made a fuss to show everybody how proud she was of me. But it would do. Main thing was I liked that feeling of belonging. I'd do anything to keep that feeling.

Next morning Mama had the bad head so I decided to fix my own hair in that new way. I tried to do like Mama'd done 'cause I wanted so much to be more like the white girls. To get that feeling of belonging again. I tied my hair with string in two ponytails on either side of my head. Only it didn't hang down in nice silky looking locks like theirs' did or even in pretty coils like when Mama fixed it. My hair stuck out from either side of my skull like two bird's nests that had blown up from a tornado or dynamite. I guess I looked pretty frightful. Only when I got to school nobody seemed frightened. Everybody looked shocked for a second or two then laughed like my head was the funniest thing they ever saw in their lives.

"What are those rat's nests doing on top your head, Scary Mary?" one boy shouted.

The other kids pointed at my hair and laughed so hard it seemed like their sides would split right open. Only it was my heart that split open instead. Split like somebody'd taken a knife to it and made a big bleeding wound. And it hurt that much too.

"Looks like the rat's nest blew up!" another boy said.

I managed to hold in my tears till three o'clock. But soon as I got home I ran down to the basement and fell facedown on the cot, the cot that still smelled like Grandpa. Then I cried and cried because they made fun of my hair.

And I was ashamed of myself. Why should a silly thing like hair make anybody cry? Or maybe *I* was what they thought was silly. It was just my hairdo that made them think it. That was even more hurtful.

All I could do to heal the hurt was practice and practice because at least then I'd get some approval. From Daddy Fletcher and Max anyway. And the teacher ladies. I just knew Miss Milholland's faith in me had to come to something sooner or later. I couldn't get out of my head what she'd said about the caul. How it meant I was destined for greatness. I didn't know about the greatness but I sure hoped it also meant the spooks would go away. I was tired of the kids at school calling me Scary Mary. They thought I was weird and I guess I didn't blame them. Nobody but me had such strange visions. Visions like the Ghost Dog.

I hadn't asked Nanny about that frightful thing for a long time because I couldn't abide the way she fussed at me about it. Used to be she'd tell me the story of the Ghost Dog like it was a special secret between her and me. But not anymore. Now she made me feel like I come from the devil 'cause of my spooky visions. And because of my music. Oh my how that hurt. I figured Mama felt the same way, though it was harder to tell because of the gin. Most things she said were fuzzy and didn't come across clear.

Like when I'd come home busting with tears after my special tea party. Mama was in the kitchen with the gin jug as usual. When I asked her why she didn't come all she said was, "Don't got no need to go to some gladragging white folks's tea party," or something like that. Her words were so fuzzed up I couldn't tell for sure. Funny how the fuzzy things folks say can hurt as much as the clear things.

22

The Garden

"Mary Mary quite contrary."

I knew that was Nanny's voice but what she said sure had me puzzled.

"What do you mean, Nanny?"

"I mean you acting contrary like you always do."

"What does contrary mean?"

"It mean you don't know how to get on with folks."

"But I do, Nanny! That's what I want more than anything. To get on with folks and bring all different kinds of people together with my music."

"Bring folks together my foot. Too full of your own self you is. Like I says, you're Mary Mary quite contrary."

"Nanny, I never heard you say a thing like that before."

"It's from a poem. I never knowed much about books, but I remember that rhyme."

"How does the rest of it go?"

"I can't right remember most of it. But let's see . . . Mary Mary, quite contrary, how does your garden grow? That's all I remember."

"Now that you've told me the rest I think I like that poem, Nanny."

"And why's that, Missy?"

"Because it's about growing a garden. And that's what my music is to me. All the time I spend at the piano is like planting seeds I hope will grow into beautiful flowers. A whole garden of beautiful flowers. I think that's what the Mary in the poem is trying to do. Only people don't know it and think she's being contrary."

Seemed Nanny didn't know what to say to this. She scrunched her mouth and stalked on back in the kitchen. I was sorry she didn't understand. I didn't want her to think I was being contrary. I wanted her to appreciate the garden I was trying to grow. It was a garden grown from love and all the fine things that come to me from the Good Spirit.

I told myself it didn't matter what Nanny thought about my music 'cause Miss Milholland said my musical ability was outstanding. And she was a smart lady and a teacher and knew what she was talking about. Not that Nanny wasn't smart but she was backward in her thinking. She pondered too much about the devil and such. Like Max said, she's from the old times.

But it still hurt that she thought my music was wicked. It hurt because my music was *me*. It came from me and was wrapped up in my whole self. It *was* my whole self. More than any other part of me. So when my own grandmother said my music's wicked and from the devil that's the same as saying *I'm* wicked and from the devil.

I knew Mama thought this too because I was born with the caul. But Miss Milholland said the caul was a gift. A gift that meant I was destined for greatness. If only what she said could be true! I wanted to believe it but Nanny and Mama's fussing about my music gave me doubts. How I wished Miss Milholland's kind words could take away those doubts.

But it's not easy when the doubts are brought about by family. They're my blood and you can't get away from blood. Least that's what Grandpa always told me. And I never doubted what Grandpa said. He was so wise. I wanted him back so bad. Sometimes the wanting was so strong it hurt worse than any whuppin Mama ever gave me.

23

The Dare

One smoggy afternoon I came home from playing piano for the teacher ladies wearing my finest dress and clutching my handkerchief full of coins. The winter air was right chilly but I had my shabby old coat slung over my arm 'cause I hated wearing it. Amy Frank was waiting for me. She sat on a wooden crate somebody'd left on the sidewalk swinging her legs and wearing her terrible smile.

"Maybe you can pound on a piano, but I dare you to jump over this box," she said.

At that she hopped to her feet and skipped a ways down the sidewalk, her yellow curls bouncing right along with her. Then with a fearsome look in her eye she broke into a run and took a flying leap clear over that crate.

"I dare you to do that," she said again with her hands on her hips and a smirky smile on her face.

I looked down at my pretty dress and had my doubts. But I couldn't let Amy show me up so I took the dare. I dropped my coat to the ground but held tight to my coins. Then I took a running leap but instead of sailing over that box like Amy did the hem of my dress caught on a sharp corner. I went crashing to the concrete and my afternoon's earnings went clattering all over the sidewalk. I managed to break my fall with my left arm but I was still in great pain as I struggled to my feet and scrambled around to gather what I could of my scattered fortune.

Amy watched me with her smirking face then skipped back to her house. My arm was bloody and sore and my dress was ruined. I ran into my house before anybody else could see me, stashed my money in its secret place and spent the rest of the afternoon hiding in the basement. I just knew if Mama found me this way she'd give me the worst whuppin of my life.

She didn't find me though. Daddy Fletcher did and he picked me up and held me on his lap till I stopped whimpering. Then I blurted out the story of what had happened.

He folded his arms around me even more tenderly. "You just lookin' for love, ain't you, Baby Doll?"

At this I felt the tears rise up in my eyes all over again.

"You just keep at your music," he said quietly. "The music you play has healing in it, and a lot of love. Can't nobody take that away from you."

That little piece of kindness on Daddy Fletcher's part was like soothing balm to a flaming wound. And he'd called me Baby Doll which he hadn't done in a long time. It felt mighty good even if my poor arm hurt so bad I thought I'd pass out. But it was worth it to be in Daddy Fletcher's arms and feel his love.

"Land sakes, what's this?"

My body did a little jerk at the sound of Nanny's voice. I hadn't heard her come down to the basement.

"Now don't you be chidin' the girl," Daddy Fletcher said. "She took a tumble out on the pavement, is all."

"I'm not chidin' her," Nanny said, breathing heavy from the climb down the stairs. "I just came to see what all the blubbering was about. Is something hurting you, child?"

"My arm, Nanny," I whimpered. "It hurts to move my arm."

"Let me have a look," she said.

I howled in pain when she lifted my arm.

"Well no wonder," she said, "this arm's broke. Now

you just hold still on your stepdaddy's lap while I go find something to bandage it up."

Nanny huffed and puffed her way back up the basement stairs and before I knew it she was back with a bucket of water and cake of soap and pile of rags. Daddy Fletcher held me firm while she scrubbed the blood and dirt off my arm then wrapped it tight in clean rags. I thought I'd die from the pain but by the time Nanny had my arm bandaged and tied in a sling it hardly hurt at all.

"Fletcher, you carry her on upstairs," Nanny said, "so's I can cut that filthy dress off her and get her into bed."

"No, Nanny!" I wailed. "This is my only nice dress!"

"It's ruined now, child. Can't be helped."

My ruined dress wasn't my worst problem. Turned out I couldn't go to school or even play piano for quite some time. After a couple weeks I began to worry that maybe I'd never be able to play piano again. Losing my music playing ability was the worst thing I could imagine except for losing Max. I fell into the bluest mood I'd ever known. Darkness flooded my mind and blotted out the comfort my music had brought to my heart.

I tried to think about what Daddy Fletcher said. How the music in my mind and in my heart had healing in it and a lot of love. Bad thing was I'd lost the power to bring my music to life. And the music stuck inside me turned dark and scary like the demons that had always haunted me. The devil was in that music like Nanny said. Oh how I fretted about this fearsome music that was suddenly haunting me from the inside.

One good thing was all the attention I got from my family. Even Mama sat by my bed from time to time. I never would have expected that. She didn't say much but she also didn't drink gin while she sat with me which almost made it worth getting my arm broke.

Then something else happened I never expected. Neighbors who always used to give me cross looks came by our house and asked why they hadn't heard me play piano lately. I never realized my music had been changing how they felt about me. Even Amy's mama liked me now. When she found out how I hurt my arm she gave me a dress in place of my ruined one. It was one of Amy's favorites and her mama marched her over to my house to make amends and give me the dress. I hoped this would be the end of Amy's grudge against me. But when I looked in her blue eyes they were fiercer than ever, and so full of hate.

WHEN NANNY FINALLY TOOK the bandages off my arm I felt panic and wondered if I'd be able to play piano. Daddy Fletcher made me go to the piano right away and try. It hurt a might at first but every day the hurting got less and less.

Funny how my broken arm made my relations take a turn of mind to my music. One day Nanny even said to me, "Go on now, go on," waving her hand t'wards the parlor. "You practice your music. It'll help get some strength back in that arm." Seemed Nanny was changing her mind about my music.

I wasn't looking to just change people's minds with my music. I wanted to change their hearts. That was my dream. What my soul hankered for more than anything. Because if people could change their hearts they could see past each other's differences and love folks for their true selves.

But my family was interested in my music for another reason. That reason was money which gave me mixed-up feelings. On the one hand I was glad my family thought highly enough about my music that they believed it could help them not be so poor. But on the other hand I was sad my family didn't see the real value of my music. In my mind that true value was a special quality that could make bridges like the train trestle Grandpa showed me back in Atlanta. Bridges that could bring people together. People like me and Mama.

And also like me and Amy Frank. I really and truly didn't hate her. I wanted her to understand me. If my music could make Amy understand me then I'd know my music could bring colored and white folks together in a special way. But for the time being it was maybe enough that my neighbors and the teachers at school appreciated my piano playing. And my family saw value in my music even if all they saw was money value. I decided for now I'd have to make do with that. Even if Max was staying away from me.

Truth was he hadn't been around to see me since before my arm got broke. I had a notion it was 'cause of his mama, seeing that her and my mama didn't get on. But whatever the reason I felt like my heart was breaking just like my arm had. I was starting to realize that without Max nothing else much mattered.

24

Mr. Rose

Soon as my arm healed I didn't have much time to think about Max. Now that my family realized I could make money as an entertainer they started lining up professional gigs for me. I believe Daddy Fletcher was the one put in charge of this, and he even bought me a brand-new coat in the latest wrap-over style. So's I'd look more presentable he said.

My very first job was with an undertaker. His name was Mr. Peyton Rose and he lived a short ways from us. Problem was Mr. Rose's funeral parlor was kind of creepy. I had to sit at this little organ that was in the same room with an open coffin playing church hymns.

First time I played there the old man in the coffin gave me the heebie jeebies. He looked like he was made of wax. And right by the coffin was a fat lady dressed all in black with a lacy veil over her face, pounding her big bosom and wailing like there was no tomorrow. Folks hardly could hear me play for the racket she made.

You'd think this would have confounded my mind and my fingers but truth was it helped. The fat lady's grieving added some pitiful feeling to my organ playing that maybe wouldn't have been there if she wasn't bawling so hard.

When I took a little pause between hymns another lady who wasn't so out of sorts came over to me. "Child, your organ playing's as glorious as the music of the prophetess Miriam in the Good Book," she said.

"Why thank you, ma'am." I didn't know what else to say. I'd never been compared to a lady prophet before.

After that first job for Mr. Rose he had me back often. But his funeral parlor didn't get any less frightful for me since I was inclined to see ghosts hovering about. Once while I was playing the organ real soft by the open coffin I could swear I heard the dead man talking to me. He said, "Little gal, play me my favorite church hymn, Rock of Ages."

I started playing the hymn without even thinking and don't you know that dead man smiled at me? I near jumped out of my skin it scared me so bad. But I kept playing all the same even though my whole body was shivering.

"Are you cold, honey?" a lady asked me.

"No ma'am," I said while I kept playing the hymn.

It worried me that folks could see how scared I was. I was afraid they'd think I had stage fright and then Mr. Rose wouldn't ask me to come play for his guests anymore. That would make Mama and Daddy Fletcher madder than hornets 'cause we needed the money so bad. So I bit my lip and breathed deep as I could to calm my fears. And I just played and played one hymn after another. All the hymns I'd ever learned from Mama's church playing so many years ago.

Before long my fears just stealed away. Like in the old slave spiritual Grandpa taught me. I started to play that spiritual on Mr. Rose's organ and hummed along while I thought of the words:

> *Steal away, steal away,*
> *Steal away to Jesus!*
> *Steal away, steal away home,*
> *I ain't got long to stay here.*

People all around me were crying.

An old man shuffled over to the organ. "That just be the near prettiest thing I ever did hear," he said, his lips smiling just a little. He reminded me of Grandpa which made my eyes water.

I played the song again, this time even softer, and the old man's smile got more gentle and sad. I saw a little tear trickle down his cheek. But he was still smiling.

MR. ROSE'S FUNERAL HOME wasn't the only place I got gigs. Soon Mamie started taking me with her when she met up with her teenage friends and I played the piano for tips. At one of these gatherings who should I run into but Amy Frank. I was surprised to see her hanging around with older girls and boys and her being there made me real nervous. So I didn't play too good. The girls were so hip. All got up in the new flapper style with their dresses above their knees, short-cut hair and painted faces. They made me feel like a pitiful ragamuffin with my hand-me-down dress and wiry braids. I saw Amy and her friends whispering and laughing while I played which made me feel even worse.

So I was real surprised when one of the older girls Amy was with came over to me later and said, "You wanna play piano at my house next Friday night? I'm having a party. My mama'll pay you."

"Why sure," I said and was I ever pleased. Amy must be mighty popular to have such swanky friends, I thought. So being asked to play at one of their parties was a real honor. And profitable too which I was glad of since that might help make Mama a little happier with me. And what a profit it was. The dollars added up faster than I could count.

After I played piano at Amy's friend's house the offers to play at parties kept coming and the tip money kept rolling in. This made me happy because I got lots of friendly smiles for this. Mama even smiled at the sight of the money I brought home. But only for a short while. Soon as she opened the gin bottle her sadness came back. And her meanness.

25

The Doll Dance

After a time Amy and her flapper friends started to find me work at more sordid places. The kinds of places that gave me the willies. One of those places was a ramshackle old house in the neighborhood that was real mysterious. Shifty-eyed men would come and go there often.

One day Amy and her buddies took me to this place and introduced me to a light-skinned Negro lady with a painted face and a dress cut low enough so's to make men's eyes pop right out of their heads. The lady had a meanness about her mouth that put me in mind of my mama I'm sorry to have to say.

I had a mind to turn on my heel and run the other way but Amy grabbed my arm and squeezed it real tight. Then she whispered in my ear. "You better stay put or I'll make you take off that dress." I had no doubt she meant this. The dress Mrs. Frank gave me had been Amy's favorite. Now it was *my* favorite and I had no aim to give it back.

The lady looked down at me, a fist propped on her plump hip. "Well, well, what we got here?"

"Why don't you introduce her," I heard one of the girls whisper to Amy.

"This here's Mary, the little piano girl of East Liberty," Amy said. That's the name folks around the neighborhood had started to call me. The name I was getting famous for. "She'll play the piano real good for you. Keep your customers entertained, you know."

The lady peered at me all wary-eyed and said nothing. Just pressed her lips together. Finally she said, "Child, you ought not to be here. This ain't the place for younguns."

"She's older than she looks," said Amy. "Don't you worry, she'll be fine. Just let her play the piano. She's real good."

"Well . . . I reckon I could give her a try," the lady said, shaking her head. I could tell she was real doubtful.

The lady led me through a door into a little room with

a rickety old piano. On another door there was a sort of peep hole and through that door I could hear a lot of strange noises. Moaning and such. The lady told me to play for the duration of the moaning.

"You best live up to all them white girls says about you," she said, shaking her finger at me. "And you best not be doing no peeking."

I nodded my head and stared at the floor. The way the lady peered at me was scary and I tried hard to keep from looking at her face. But I did as she told me and played some blues tunes, trying to stretch out the tunes for the duration of the moaning like the lady said. The duration went on and on. I started to get mad because my hands were getting tired. And Amy and the other girls had taken off and left me all alone in this spooky place.

It finally got so late I stopped playing and tried to sneak out. But the lady with the painted face seemed to show up out of nowhere. She put her hands on her hips and frowned down at me. "Just where do you think you're going, miss?"

Her sharp glare was downright frightful so I figured I had no choice but to stay and do like she said. After she left again I sat and sat and played piano till I thought my hands would fall off. I wanted so bad to go find Amy and the other girls. They were probably waiting for me outside. But just thinking about the look on the painted lady's face made a big knot in me that kept me tied to that piano. Till the lady finally came back to fetch me.

"Ain't nobody waitin' on you," she said. "You best be gettin' on home." She didn't say it in any too friendly a way. But she did give me ten dollars which of course I'd have to share with the other girls. It would only be fitting since they'd gotten me the gig.

The lady was right that the girls weren't waiting for me. And Pittsburgh's early dusk had already fallen over the neighborhood. I hardly could see where I was going. As I walked by a little church cemetery I remembered the story Nanny had so often told back in Georgia about the Ghost Dog. How so many had seen it leap out of the steamy marshes or the dark woods along the dirt road that passed by the old graveyard.

No sooner had this frightful story worried my mind when I spotted a fluffy little white dog peak at me from behind one of the gravestones. The pup started to scamper toward me in a friendly sort of way, wagging its tail. Then before my very eyes it turned into the hugest most terrifying white furry creature I could ever imagine! Its red eyes blazed like torches and drool dripped from its yellow fangs. Like some crazed animal I ran with a frenzy till I reached my house.

Mama sat on the front step glaring at me. Her mouth was tight and mean like the lady in the ramshackle house. And she reeked of gin. Without saying a word she made my bones rattle and visions of the Ghost Dog rose in my head again. I started to get the sinking feeling that comes when you know something bad's about to happen.

"I been a-waitin' on you. Where you been?" she asked, her voice cold as winter ice.

I was still shivering with fright from the Ghost Dog. And the ice in Mama's voice made me shake even more. But I tried to hold onto the hope that she'd understand and comfort me. I ran to her, grabbed her hand and babbled out the story of the fearsome dog.

She jerked her hand from mine and slapped me. "How come you always cookin' up trouble and making this family look bad? You been playing piano at that filthy whorehouse. Miss Amy next door tell me so. And now you come home full of lies about your fool ghosts and visions."

Rage boiled up in me but I wouldn't let myself cry. With Mama I'd learned it's best if I don't carry on when I'm boiling up.

Mama grabbed my arm. Then she picked up a long twig from the ground and swatted the backs of my legs till they felt like they were on fire.

I DIDN'T SLEEP THAT NIGHT. Each time I closed my eyes I saw a monstrous white face, its eyes filled with fire, hovering over my bed and leering at me.

Tired and sore, I loped to the parlor early next morning and sat at my piano. I pretended the piano was a dollhouse. My fingers were the dolls and they were free to do whatever they wanted. Free as little birds fluttering in the morning sunlight. All this was happening in my head but that didn't matter. In my head I was free.

So I just stayed in my head that day and played with my made-up dollhouse till I made my very own song. I decided to call it The Doll Dance because the tune was like a waltz. The song was sweet but also sad since the dolls in my head danced to forget their hurt. I played that song over and over till it was perfect. And while I played I forgot my own hurt too.

I'd never had my own doll. Not that I ever wanted one. I liked things that were real or at least that seemed real. Like the toy train with the real boiler Grandpa made me. But not some fake person. Not one of those dolls with rubber faces and big shiny dead eyes to dress up and take for buggy rides. Toys like that weren't real and didn't even seem real.

The dolls in my head lived and breathed and danced 'cause they were happy and free. My music made the dolls in my head real, because my music was the only part of me that was happy and free.

26

Fear

That evening I felt tingly happy waiting for Daddy Fletcher to come home from the laboring yard, even if my legs still stung from the whipping Mama'd given me the day before. I couldn't wait to play him the Doll Dance song I'd been working on all day.

My back hurt from sitting at the piano so long but I couldn't make myself move away from it. It was the safest place in the house and the only place I could really be myself. That's 'cause my fingers were free to tell the story of my feelings and fears even if my voice wasn't.

Daddy Fletcher understood about my music. I knew

this because he'd spent so much of the money he won at cards to buy me my very own piano. And he'd taught me about the blues. What a wonderful feeling it was to know he loved me that much. As wonderful as having my own real daddy. Maybe even better.

My heart got bouncy with excitement and relief when I finally heard him come in the front door. But a second later my fingers froze from the chill he brought into the room. I looked up at him from the piano bench and he gave me a scowly look that sent a shiver right through me. He glared at me a minute then turned his head to the side and spit once like he always did when he was mad. That's how everybody knew to get out of his way.

This time I didn't get out of his way. I was too weighed down by the sadness and dread that had suddenly filled my whole body and froze me to the bench.

"Get yourself off that piano bench and go help your mama fix my supper," he said.

I could tell he'd been at the bottle. Burning tears crept into to my eyes and the dread grew more powerful.

"What you waitin' for, girl? Git in the kitchen like I said."

I slipped off the bench with shaking knees and a heart that felt like it was sinking to the soles of my feet. "But . . ." I started to say. I didn't want to go in the kitchen. I knew there was no supper being fixed. Only gin being drunk. And I didn't want to be the one to tell that to Daddy Fletcher.

He strode closer to me in a threatening way. I stared at my feet. I couldn't abide the cold mean look in his eyes.

"I told you to get in the kitchen!"

I was shaking so bad I hardly could move. But somehow my shaking legs managed to run to the kitchen. Mama looked up from the table where she sat with Nanny, her eyes hazy from the gin.

"Daddy Fletcher wants his supper," I said in a soft trembly voice.

Mama's eyes spit fire. I knew before she had a chance to say a word trouble was coming. In fear I turned and ran down the basement stairs to the place where Grandpa and me used to have our special time. I curled up on Grandpa's cozy little bed and pretended he was there with me. I could hear Daddy Fletcher's feet scuffling around on the kitchen floor above. Then the shouting started. And the vicious name calling. I covered my ears but the ugly sounds still came through in a muffled way.

I closed my eyes tight as I could but that didn't stop the vision that loomed before me. The Ghost Dog, its fur standing up straight and its big sharp teeth bared, was lunging towards me. And weren't my insides ever jumping. I curled up in a ball, wrapped my arms around my head and waited for the attack.

THE ATTACK NEVER CAME but the feeling of terror the Ghost Dog's fierce eyes brought to my heart didn't go away. More and more Daddy Fletcher would look at me with a scary sort of grin that made my skin crawl. He'd been so nice before Grandpa died, encouraging me in my music and all. And then for a time when my arm broke. But now he scared me. He'd taken more and more to drinking gin with Mama and Nanny and I knew from the beginning that could lead to nothing good. Just like Mama, he got mean when he drank.

To make things worse his Georgia Skin games hadn't been doing too good either. He'd been on what he called a losing streak which put him in a bad temper. He even stopped taking me with him to the gambling joint 'cause he said I was bringing him bad luck.

Whenever I let myself think about how kind and loving Daddy Fletcher used to be it hurt so bad I hardly could stand it. I felt jilted of his love and the loneliness that made me feel was like a dark hole with no way out. I thought about Grandpa in his dark hole that was his grave and my heart ached so bad I was afraid I'd keel right over and die like him. Music was my only escape. Thank the Lord I still had my player piano. Even if Daddy Fletcher sometimes threatened to sell it when he needed money for gambling.

That threat became real one day when Daddy Fletcher near made me jump out of my skin. "Git away from that thing. A man's coming to give me a price for it," he said as he staggered out of the kitchen clutching a mug of gin in his fist.

I balled up my hands in my lap and hung my head while tears started to run down my cheeks. "Please, Daddy Fletcher, please don't sell my piano. I can't live without it."

"*Your* piano? Who in tarnation you think paid for it? That be *my* piano, girlie, and I'm ordering you to remove your little behind from that stool right now, 'less you wanna have the devil to pay." His words were slurry and it seemed like he could hardly stay standing.

He spat on the floor, scowling mad. Scared as I was I wouldn't budge. No matter what kinds of threatening things came out of Daddy Fletcher's mouth I felt sure he'd never lay a hand on me. But his words hurt more than any slap. He kept glaring at me, trying to cow me I guess, till I stared him down with my sad eyes. Then he stomped back in the kitchen, to pour another mug of gin I reckon.

As if Daddy Fletcher turning mean wasn't bad enough Mama got worse too. Lately she'd took to hiding behind the locked door of her bedroom. Daddy Fletcher would explain, "Your mama got a headache this morning," or "Your mama don't feel too good. She be out in a while."

She threw up sometimes on those days. I saw this once when Daddy Fletcher forgot to lock the bedroom door. I heard Mama making terrible noises and when I crept to her door I saw the blood she'd gagged up. Bright red and thick in the bucket by her bed.

And when she wasn't gagging up blood she'd use what little strength she had to give me a beating whenever it suited her. Seemed like I got beat every day for some reason or another. Most times for no reason at all 'cept Mama had the bad head and couldn't abide me being around.

After one of those beatings I crept down to the basement trying not to let the tears fall. I pulled the Beethoven book from under Grandpa's cot. The one Miss Milholland gave me. The book was a comfort to me because it said Beethoven got beat too when he was a boy. Just like with me it was for no reason except that his daddy drank too much wine and got in a temper. The misery this caused in him, and his deafness, made such a loneliness in him. *I must live almost alone, like one who has been banished*, he wrote to his brothers.

But Beethoven did wonderful things with his music in spite of all that. *Music was his protection and his refuge*, the book said, *then and to the end of his days*. Even though he was going deaf. It was the worst thing that could happen to somebody like Beethoven. The deafness made him think about killing himself but his music saved him and he wanted to share that. He wanted to make everybody in the world feel like brothers and he almost did I think. That's what I wanted too.

27

Mrs. Mellon

The very next Sunday afternoon a long black automobile pulled up in front of my house. I was at the piano and saw it through the parlor window. It was the biggest automobile I ever saw and I ran to the door and stood on the front step gaping.

A colored man in a fine suit and black hat with a shiny visor stepped out of the automobile and grinned at me. He tipped his hat. "Are you the little piano girl?" he said.

"Yes sir, I do play piano," I said, my eyes wide with wonder.

"My employer, Mrs. Mellon, would like to hire you to

play piano at her bridge party."

I felt like I couldn't breathe. Finally I managed to breathe in real deep. "When?" I asked.

"Why this very afternoon, miss."

I couldn't hardly believe it. I'd heard about Mrs. Mellon. Everybody knew about her. She was the richest lady in Pittsburgh. And she wanted me to play piano at her house that very afternoon. I just knew Miss Milholland had been the one to set this up. Quick as I could I ran in the house and changed into my good dress, the one Amy's mama made her give me. Then I grabbed my coat and ran back toward the front door.

"Where you think you're going, missy?" Nanny had just stepped out of the kitchen and was wiping her hands on a dish rag.

"Gotta go, Nanny! I got a gig!" I screeched as I ran past her.

Before Nanny could say another word I was out the door. The man was still standing by the fancy automobile. He opened the back seat door and I jumped in.

What an adventure. I'd never ridden in an automobile before much less a big fancy one like this. We drove and drove till I couldn't see any more buildings and only trees. Then it seemed like we were going up, up, up. High above the smoke and slums of Pittsburgh. Finally we drove through some big iron gates and my eyes near popped from my head at the sight of the enormous house that stood before me.

The driver hopped out and opened the door for me and led me to the mansion's grand entranceway. Inside the house a colored maid led me into the biggest living room I could ever imagine and over to a long black piano. I'd never seen such a piano. But what really caught my eye was the beautiful silver-haired lady standing by that piano. She smiled at me in the nicest way.

"You must be the little piano girl of East Liberty," she said, her voice as silky as her swanky flowered dress.

"Yes, ma'am, that's what folks call me. But my real name's Mary."

She tilted her head back and gave the prettiest little laugh. "It's lovely to meet you, Mary. I'm Mrs. Mellon."

"Lovely to meet you too, Mrs. Mellon," I said, trying hard as I could not to stutter and to make my voice sound silky like hers.

Mrs. Mellon smiled her pretty smile again. "Tell me, honey, how much do you charge?"

"Oh I usually get about a dollar an hour," I said, my voice shaking just a little. I didn't want to sound too greedy.

"What I'd like you to do is play a few popular tunes for a couple of hours while I entertain my guests at bridge. Do you think you can do that?"

"Sure, ma'am. It'd be my pleasure."

Still smiling, Mrs. Mellon nodded her head then turned and went into a big room made of glass that was right off the living room. I sat at the piano with my feet dangling since they didn't quite reach the floor and looked down at the gleaming black and white keys. I let my fingers slide along their cold smoothness for a second or two then I started to play.

I played and played all my favorite tunes, Jelly Roll Morton and Scott Joplin and some of my own while the ladies in the next room laughed and chatted and clinked their tea cups and saucers. It was so pleasant in that house. I was concentrating hard on my piano playing but still managed to look around at the fine surroundings. Huge thick rugs with swirly colors covered the shiny wood floors, and paintings of serious looking people were all over the walls. With every breath the smell of fresh flowers filled my head.

At the end of the two hours Mrs. Mellon came back to the piano, thanked me and gave me an envelope. The driver took me to the car and on the way home I opened the envelope. I almost fainted. The check was for one hundred dollars. I was bubbling over with so much excitement my family's greed flew clear out of my head. Soon as we pulled up to my house and the driver opened the door for me I ran inside to show Mama.

"I been playing piano at Mrs. Mellon's house. She paid me a hundred dollars!" I said.

Mama's mouth fell open. This was more money than she ever earned in even a month with her washing and ironing.

For once Mama seemed clearheaded. She must not have been drinking gin yet that day. "You sure that what she meant to pay you?" she asked.

"Well sure I'm sure, Mama. Why else would Mrs. Mellon write that number on the check?"

But Mama was scared Mrs. Mellon had made a mistake and the police would come. So right quick she ran down to the corner drugstore where the pay telephone was. I trailed after her and heard her ask the operator to connect her with Mrs. Mellon who assured Mama there was no mistake. My family stayed up that whole night till the bank opened next morning.

After that Mrs. Mellon had me play regular for her. This pleased Mama and she started treating me so nice, smiling at me like she never had before. It was so swell that Mama finally took a liking to me and to what I aimed to do with my music. I just knew things were going to change. Now she would give me the love and praise I'd always ached for.

But I can't say she exactly gave me that feeling of love I wanted so bad. Maybe that was too much to hope for. You shouldn't expect folks to give what they don't have to give. Even your own mama. But she seemed happy with the money I was bringing her and she wasn't drinking so much. And that was good enough for now. At least she finally seemed to approve of me.

Mama's approving didn't last. One day Mrs. Mellon's driver delivered me back home and I skipped up to the front step full of happy feelings about how good my music business was going.

Mama sat there reeking of gin, her eyes hard. "Look at you, carryin' on like trash, having the fine time," she said, her voice slurry.

The sinking feeling was coming over me but I tried to talk sensible. "I'm not carrying on like trash, Mama. I been playing piano at Mrs. Mellon's house and she's a fine lady and pays good money. I thought that would make you happy."

Mama took a slug of gin and cocked her head to the side. "You gettin' the big head, ain't you? Puttin' on uppity airs, prancin' all over town playin' your devil music for them rich white folks." Her words all ran together. It was the gin talking but the hurt her words brought still tied my belly in knots.

"But Mama, I thought you liked it that I'm making money with my music."

"That don't mean nothin' when you go 'gainst the Lord's commandment."

"What do you mean, Mama? Which commandment did I go against?"

"The one that say honor thy mother."

"But—"

"You don't honor me, you never have. You think you're better than me, and that go 'gainst the word of God. You be goin' down Satan's path by and by, just like your nanny say." Mama's hard eyes stared at me.

My head was stuffed with tears. I felt my face scrunch up. "Don't say that, Mama," I finally managed to choke out through my tears. "You been drinking too much gin and you don't know what you're saying."

Mama' eyes brightened in a threatening way. "You best not be sassin' me, girl."

"No, Mama," I said real soft and tried to step past her into the house. But Mama fumbled to her feet all unsteady and staggered into the house ahead of me. I followed her hoping for some supper 'cause my belly was starting to growl.

I went to bed hungry that night. There was no food in the kitchen and Mama and Nanny were too far gone with the gin to care. When Daddy Fletcher came home and saw there was no supper he stomped out of the house saying he got better treatment at the gambling hall than he did at home.

I lay in the bed with my belly rumbling and all kinds of scary thoughts went through my head. Thoughts about Mama and how unhappy she was. Her unhappiness made my stomach curl up in agony and brought to mind the Ghost Dog. Truth was the Ghost Dog seemed like it was hovering nearby ready to pounce on me any minute.

I pulled the sheet over my head and prayed for the Ghost Dog to go away. But the feeling that he was hovering over me just kept getting worse and worse. My whole body shivered all through that fearsome night. I don't know whether I shook more from fright or from the cold sweat that soaked my night shift.

And I thought about Max. How he hadn't been around to see me for the longest time. I suddenly missed him so much I couldn't hardly stand it. I ached to feel his strong arms around me. The arms that made me feel so safe and loved. Like Grandpa always did.

The next day was Sunday and soon as I woke I went straight to the piano and played some wild sounding music. I don't know where that music came from but it just poured out through my fingers.

"Quit the racket!" Mama yelled. She had the bad head from all the drinking the night before. I felt awful about that but I knew this music just had to come out of me or I'd bust. I kept playing and playing. And Mama didn't try to stop me.

28

The Power of Music

I played piano so hard and long that morning my arms near gave out. When I stopped a minute to rest, my eyes wandered to the parlor window and my heart did a somersault. Max was standing outside the window grinning his handsome grin.

I ran out the front door and he didn't say anything but took me in his arms and held me tight.

"Sorry I haven't come around for so long," he said.

He loosed up his hold on me and I stepped back a little.

"Where've you been, Max? I thought you up and left town or something."

"I been in town. But except for going to school my mama's hardly let me out of the house for weeks."

"Why's that, Max? Has your mama been sick or something?"

"Naw, she ain't sick. She just say I been spending too much time with you and she needs me home to do chores and stuff. But I couldn't stay away any longer, Mary. I've really missed you."

The thrill that swept over me and through me was like when the Good Spirit brought music to me. But in an even more exciting way.

"I've missed you too, Max. I was afraid I'd never see you again."

He smiled at me and his eyes were so sweet and tender my insides felt like warm maple syrup.

"You're the niftiest girl I ever met," he finally said, and if my skin wasn't so dark the blush that rose up would've turned my cheeks bright red.

"You're right nifty too," I said, trying hard not to stutter.

"That music you were playing just now is something else, Mary. It's different from anything I ever heard. Your music gets to me is all I can say. It tells me there's something really special about you."

My syrupy insides sloshed and bubbled like they were fixing to spurt right out of me. I tried to breathe deep to calm the bubbling but it wouldn't stop. I wrapped my arms around Max and hugged him hard as I could.

He hugged me back and I felt his strong heartbeat and got the comforting feeling I used to get with Grandpa. But my insides never got that bubbling way with Grandpa. Only with Max. I guess that meant I was in love. Before Max I never knew what being in love felt like but I figured this must be it. It was a feeling I wanted to have forever. I was so happy to be in Max's arms again I thought just maybe I'd give up anything to feel that love forever. Even my music.

But Miss Milholland said I had such a talent and I didn't want to let her down. She said I should be working on my music all the time. And I wanted to do it. I wanted to do it for Max. He was my new inspiration, like the Good Spirit. Only Max was real flesh and blood and hard and warm and made my body tingle all over every time I looked at him. And even more when he touched me.

I thought about him when I played ragtime. That Scott Joplin music I heard on one of my piano rolls, the Pineapple Rag, really got me going. While I played I thought about eating pineapple and its sweet juiciness became so real to me I could taste it. That sweet juiciness seemed to rush through me and gave me such a wonderful feeling that I hurled my whole body into my playing. Thinking about Max made me want to do that.

My feelings about Max got all mixed up with my feelings about my music and I couldn't keep all those mixed-up feelings in. So I played on and on.

"Stop that bangin'!" Nanny yelled from the kitchen.

"I'm not banging!" I yelled back. "This is ragtime. The music come down from slavery that's full of the Good Spirit!"

"That be Satan's music," she said, walking into the parlor wiping her hands on her apron. "You best play music that be more fittin'."

"Like what, Nanny?"

"Like that nice song I sung you many a time, My Mama Pinned a Rose, you know the one."

"I do, Nanny. I love it when you sing that song. It's my favorite."

Nanny's smile was approving which was a switch from her usual look. I thought maybe Nanny finally understood about my music. I was wrong.

"You set your mind to decent songs and steer clear of that devil music."

"But Nanny, my music has power. It has healing power. And power to bring different kinds of folks together."

"You got no power, child. Don't you know poor folks got no power? 'Specially poor colored folks like us."

"But my music does. I seen it."

"What you seen is folks curious about all the racket

you make. That be the devil's way of gettin' to them. That be the devil's power, not yours, child."

"No Nanny, the power's in the music and comes from the Good Spirit and not you or anybody can tell me that's not true."

Nanny's mouth took on the hard look. "I won't stand for no wiseacre talk, you understand? Now hush up and go someplace where you won't bother nobody."

My nanny didn't take me or my music serious. But that wasn't my biggest problem. Problem was nobody took colored girls very serious. Nanny was right about that. Colored girls had no power. But my music had power 'cause it was from the Good Spirit. I knew that because of what Grandpa told me.

29

Friends

I dreamed about marrying Max one day and for quite a time that's all I ever thought about. In my mind I pictured the cozy little house we'd share, far away from smoky old Pittsburgh. A safe happy place where there was no hurt and no bad feelings. Like the doll house I'd imagined. I knew Max wanted this too. I felt so sure of his love. If I could have Max and music too that would be the best. But if I had to pick one it would sure enough be Max.

I decided we should talk about the way I felt. "I figure we'll get married some day," I said to him, real bashful.

He didn't say anything for a minute. He just looked

at me and smiled kind of sad. Finally he said, "My mama always say I can't marry no cousin, Mary. Our babies would be monsters."

Visions of adorable puppies turning into fearsome monster dogs with dripping white fangs raced through my mind. Max must have seen the look of horror on my face because he put his arms around me and held me close.

"That don't mean we can't be friends, Mary. The very best of friends. And I'll always love you. You know good as I do that's what really matters."

But I wanted to be more than just friends. I sniffled into his shoulder and nodded my head anyway so he wouldn't think I was being ornery. I didn't want to give him a reason to ever want to stay away from me again.

Later I comforted myself a little by thinking about what Max said. How if we couldn't ever be married at least we could be friends. Best friends. I'd rather be best friends with Max the rest of my life than married to somebody I didn't love. Somebody who didn't treat me right like Max always did. I decided I wouldn't be in love with Max anymore but only good friends with him. Then maybe we could be together forever.

But my hankering for him didn't go away. I thought about Max day and night and the music that came from my heart now was kind of romantic, glittery almost. My feelings for Max added something different to my piano playing. The music that danced in my heart made my fingers move in a new and exciting way and made a bright shiny kind of sound that hadn't been there before. That's because Max gave me the shivers but in a good way. Not like my frightful visions.

From then on every time I saw Max I'd hug him tight and my heart would swell with love for him. But all too soon my swelling heart withered like a prune.

"Mary," Max said to me one day with a sad look on his face. "My mama's fixing to move us to Philadelphia. We're leaving day after tomorrow. So I won't be able to see much of you no more."

It was like the bottom suddenly dropped out of my little world. I turned away from him and fought back the flood of tears busting to get out.

He turned me back around and hugged me tight. "It won't be so bad," he said. "I'll send you letters, I promise. And besides, we're cousins, right? We're family. It won't be long before we meet up again, you'll see." Then he hugged me even tighter and whispered real soft. "And don't ever stop practicing that jazz music. The way you pour so much love into your music tells me it must make you feel real good inside. And if it makes you feel good it'll make other folks feel good too."

That's exactly what I'd always thought and now Max thought the same thing. His words reminded me of what Daddy Fletcher had said. That my music had healing in it and a lot of love.

I leaned my face into Max's soft cotton shirt and breathed in the wonderful smell of him. That boy smell that was like fire and salt and laundry soap all mixed together. Then I felt his shirt get soaked with my tears. The wetness felt warm. So warm it burned my face and made me bawl all the more. Max's arms around me should have been a comfort but now they just caused me more hurt. How could he hurt me so much? All I could see was another loss. Another person I loved walking out of my life.

30

Miss Milholland

School was over for the day but I didn't want to leave.

"Is there anything you need help with, Miss Milholland?" I asked.

Miss Milholland was sitting at her desk grading papers but she stopped for a minute and smiled up at me. "Why don't you scrub down the chalkboard, Mary," she said in her cheery way.

"Why sure, Miss Milholland." I could feel my grin. My cheeks were spread so wide I thought my face would split in two.

"Have you been practicing your music much these days?" she asked.

"Not as much as I'd like." I hung my head because this was a shameful thing to admit.

She frowned a little. "Why not? You have such a talent, Mary, I'd think you'd be working on your music all the time."

"I used to." I hung my head even lower.

"And why not anymore?"

"I just don't like being at my house these days."

She looked at me in a sad sort of way. "Things have been hard at home since your grandfather died, haven't they?"

"Yes, ma'am." I didn't know what else to say. It was too shameful to admit how Mama and Nanny guzzled gin all the time and how Daddy Fletcher had turned mean. And how my heart near tore open every time I thought about Max.

Miss Milholland kept looking at me with the sad look but didn't ask me any more questions.

Then she put down her pen and sighed. "Mary, I have something to tell you."

For some reason I started to get a sickly feeling in my stomach.

"I'm getting married on March 31, the day before Easter," she said. "I haven't told any other students yet. I wanted you to be the first to know."

I felt a big rush of relief. I was so honored she'd told me before anybody else. "Why what a fine thing that is,

Miss Milholland! I'm real happy for you."

Her smile was so kind but also a little sad. "Why thank you, sugar. You're so sweet to say that."

I shuffled my feet around. "So . . . I guess you'll be moving out of the boardinghouse."

"Yes." She looked straight in my eyes and breathed real deep. "And not only that, but also out of the Pittsburgh area."

My sinking stomach felt like it was weighed down by a heavy rock. "Then . . . you won't be teaching here anymore?"

"I'm afraid not, Mary. You see, my fiancé is starting a new job in Harrisburg on April 9."

"Is Harrisburg far from here?"

"Yes, about three hundred miles to the east. Harrisburg's our state capitol, you know."

"Yes, ma'am. I know."

"Of course you do. You're such a diligent student, Mary."

"Thank you, ma'am. And you're such a good teacher. So . . . who'll our new teacher be?"

"I don't know yet. But I'm certain Lincoln School will find someone just fine to replace me."

"I sure will miss you, Miss Milholland." My voice felt so small I wasn't even sure if she heard me.

But she did hear me. "I'll certainly miss you too, Mary."

What I didn't tell her was my insides felt like a thunderstorm. I had to leave before the tears pushing against the backs of my eyes started to spurt. I forced my mouth into a smile while I picked up my schoolbooks and walked out the door.

My feet loped so slow on the walk home it seemed like I was slugging through mud. About a block from my house I came across a group of boys breaking bottles on the sidewalk. When they saw me they started laughing and throwing the bottles my way.

"Git off this street, you African goon!" one yelled.

"I'm not African. I'm American just like you," I said.

This only made them laugh even harder.

"Hey, see if you can catch this, monkey girl!" one yelled.

"I c-can't."

"You c-cant?" he shouted back, his face twisted and mocking. "What are you, brainless?" He and the other boys laughed all the louder and picked up more bottles to throw at me.

I could feel and hear the glass crunching under my feet. I was shaking so hard I could hardly move, but I crouched down low and pressed my schoolbooks to my chest and scrunched my eyes tight closed. But that didn't shield me from those boys' ugly laughing.

Nothing hit me but glass smashed all around me as I stood back up and bent my head over the books I still clutched in my arms. Stumbling through the broken bits, I lost my balance. I hit the ground then scrambled to my feet again fast as I could. As I pushed off the pavement a pain sharp and biting shot through my hand. I started to run and kept running even though the pain leaping from my hand was like fire. I ran home so fast I hardly could feel my feet touch the ground.

Mama was at the kitchen table when I came in the back door. She smelled like gin and sweat. I dropped my books on the table and held out my bleeding hand to her. I couldn't hardly breathe 'cause of the sobs bubbling inside me.

"I got no time to be bothered with you right now," she said.

I sobbed all the harder from the awful pain as I scuffed off to my bedroom. I'd of rather gone to the basement where at least I might feel the comfort of Grandpa's spirit. But I was hurting so much I didn't even think I could make it down the stairs. It wasn't my hand that hurt at that moment though. It was my heart.

Why don't you love me, Mama? I wailed on the inside. Mamas are supposed to take care of their little girls' hurts and hug and kiss their pain away. Instead she made my hurt worse. I didn't know what hurt more—the bottle-throwing boys out on the sidewalk or Mama not caring about it. Mama was just as hateful as those boys.

All that hurting made me want Max so much I thought I'd shrivel up and die inside. And now with Miss Milholland leaving I didn't know how I could bear all the hurting and missing. And Grandpa. I wanted him back so bad. He was the only one who ever made me feel completely safe and protected. He was so wise and always knew the right story to tell me to help me climb out of my bad feelings. Those stories fed my soul and my music. I tried to talk to him in my mind but all I heard back was silence. The silence only made my grief worse.

"What devilry you been up to now, girl?" Nanny was standing at my bedroom door, her hands on her hips.

I looked over at her from my bed where I was laying. "I hurt my hand, Nanny. It hurts real bad."

She came over to take a closer look. "I should say it do. That be quite a gash you got there." She sighed. Her aggravated sigh. "Let me go get some unguent and rags," she said as she shuffled back out of the room.

When Nanny came back she didn't ask how I hurt my hand. She just frowned and kept shaking her head while she cleaned and bandaged it. The hurt eased up some but the tears wouldn't stop gushing out of my eyes.

"Now stop your bawlin'," she said, but in a gentle way.

"I just miss Grandpa so much," I blurted out.

Nanny had no patience with my grieving. She sighed again. "Child, your grandpa done gone to glory, and you best quit your mopin'. What might he say if he saw you carrying on like this?"

"What would he say, Nanny?" My head was so stuffed and my voice so shaky I hardly could talk.

"He'd say you should play that piano. Soon as this hand heals up, which shouldn't be too long. The cut's not deep as I thought. So soon as you can manage it you get back to your practicing. That what your grandpa always loved for you to do."

"But you always say my music sounds like racket, Nanny."

"I reckon that jazz music ain't so bad. I'm guessin' I changed my mind about it."

I was right pleased Nanny had another turn of mind about my music, like she did after my arm broke. And this time I had a notion she really meant it. Maybe Grandpa going to glory had finally sunk in and changed her thinking. I felt my tears dry up a little.

Then my eyes got burning wet again. "But Nanny, Daddy Fletcher wants to sell my piano 'cause of his losing streak."

Nanny folded her arms and her mouth got tight. Her cross look. "I knowed that man was a no-count the minute I laid eyes on him. But no-count or not he give you that piano as a gift and he best not be taking it back. Not while I got breath in my body."

I thought about how nice Daddy Fletcher used to be and my eyes got even more wet with tears. "Why's he turned so mean?" I asked Nanny.

She shook her head and said you never know with men. "They does what they pleases," she said.

Sometimes Nanny's crossness made me feel safe and this was one of those times. I blinked away the wetness in my eyes and smiled at her.

"Now soon as that hand heals you get back to your practicing like I told you. You know that's what your grandpa'd want."

I never thought I'd hear such words from Nanny long as I lived. Truth was her words lifted my spirits more than they'd ever been lifted since Grandpa passed to glory. Maybe that meant I was finally ready to move on with my music. I hoped that's what it meant. And for the first time since Max left town I got filled with music and was itching to get it out.

For that reason I thought real careful about what Nanny said. I remembered what Grandpa told me about music and the Good Spirit. If the spirit of music could help the slaves in their despair then surely it could help me now in my misery. And maybe Nanny's too. Even if she wouldn't own up to how much misery she felt since Grandpa'd gone to glory.

Then I remembered the book I'd read about Beethoven. How he was the greatest piano player around but then he lost his hearing. Went completely deaf. The book said after that he wrote his greatest music. I thought again about how Beethoven must have suffered with his deafness and the amazing music that came out of that suffering. Just like spirituals came out of the slaves' suffering and led the way to jazz.

I got out one of my old piano rolls, one I hadn't listened to for a long time. Beethoven's Pathétique Sonata. Grandpa loved that music and now I knew why. The name meant the music had come from Beethoven's deepest feelings and sufferings, the book said. And that's the way it was with the slaves and their spirituals.

While I listened to Beethoven I thought about Grandpa and our special talks. The talks that always gave me such a safe feeling. I just listened and listened until that safe feeling started to creep back into my heart.

Then I kept listening and the safe feeling in my heart grew bigger and more powerful. It was like Grandpa was with me again, like he'd become part of the Good Spirit. And that's what saved me from my grief over missing Grandpa. And Miss Milholland. And Max.

31

Hugh Floyd

By Easter my hand was all healed and I was back to playing piano which I had lots of time for because of the weeklong holiday. But I knew when I went back to school Miss Milholland wouldn't be there anymore. And there was no way the new teacher would be as pretty and sweet and kind as Miss Milholland. Easter night I felt so bad I couldn't sleep so I got out of bed and went to the parlor to try to work out my feelings on the piano.

It was late and the parlor was so dark I couldn't hardly see a thing. But I heard funny noises. I turned on the lamp and saw Mamie and her boyfriend Hugh on the couch kissing. They both kind of jumped when the light went on.

Mamie looked at me real cross, her lips pressed tight. "You're not supposed to be in here. Now get on out."

I felt so crushed inside. Like my best friend had just turned on me for no reason. My eyes got salty wet and I ran from the room. I went down to the basement and curled up on Grandpa's old bed. I could still smell the scent of him and that smell made my tears gush out even faster.

"I'M LEAVING, MAMA," Mamie announced later that week.

"What you mean, you leavin'? Where you think you going?" Mama asked, her words slurred by drink.

"I'm getting married." Mamie lifted her chin like she was making a dare.

Mama's eyes near popped out of her head. "You can't get married, girl! You just a baby."

Mamie rolled her eyes and sighed. "Don't even start, Mama. I'm getting out of this house of horrors before it swallows me whole."

Before Mama could say another word Mamie sashayed on back to her room. I was right at her heels.

"Who you gonna marry, Mamie? Is it that cute sax player Hugh Floyd?"

Mamie right near preened. "Sure is. You already knew, didn't you, Mary? You always know these things."

I smiled. "Well I had a strong feeling. 'Specially after I saw y'all smooching in the parlor that night."

I was real happy for Mamie just like I'd been happy for Miss Milholland. But I didn't know how I could abide living in my mama's house without Mamie there. Where could I go, though? There was no place. Max had moved away and I had no other real friends. Only people who pretended they liked me so they could hear my music.

Strange how people liked my music but not me. That's what was different about Max. He liked my music *and* me but I think he liked me just a little bit better. Funny how that thought put me in mind of Grandpa. He loved me and my music too but loved me a little better. Maybe a lot better.

Maybe liking my music was the same as liking *me*, in a roundabout sort of way. Even if that was true it still didn't fix the problem of where else I could ever live except Mama's house. There was no doubt about it. I was stuck. And I sure didn't like it one bit. I'd do about anything to get away from that house. I needed to get out to create. And to breathe.

Later that day I finally got up the nerve to talk to Mamie about my problem. She was sitting at her dressing table fussing with her lipstick. The bright red kind that smells like cherries. I stood at her bedroom door shuffling my feet.

"Mamie?"

"Yeah?" She was staring in the mirror with her mouth open, spreading the lipstick real slow and careful.

I paused and looked down at my shoes. "I don't think I can live in this house anymore without you here."

"Where would you live then?" She smacked her lips to even out the lipstick.

I shuffled my feet some more. "Could I . . . do you think . . . I could move in with you and Hugh?" I looked up at her face in the mirror, my eyes hopeful.

Mamie put down her lipstick and kept staring in the mirror for a minute. Then she turned around to face me. "I don't know, Mary. I mean, Hugh and me don't even know for sure where we're gonna live yet. It'll probably be a real small place."

"I don't care. All I need is a little corner or something to curl up in."

She folded her arms and narrowed her eyes. Her serious look. "Let me think about it."

"Oh please, Mamie. Don't leave me here."

Mamie's red-painted lips got tight like they always did when I took on like that. "Hush up, now, I'm thinking."

I stayed quiet but I couldn't stand still. I hopped from one foot to the other.

I thought Mamie would get real cross. But she surprised me and all of a sudden smiled in a kindly way like she felt sorry for me.

"I'll talk to Hugh," she said.

CAN YOU BELIEVE HUGH agreed to let me live with Mamie and him? He'd found a little house for them over on Winfield Street which was only about five minutes from Mama's house. He said he could afford the rent because of all his sax-playing gigs. After that he and Mamie got married right quick. In a place called a wedding chapel they said. Didn't matter where to me 'cause I was so happy I almost felt like I got married too. Before long Hugh became the new most important man in my life. He called me "Mary Berry" which was his way of saying he thought I was real swell.

Hugh and some of his music friends moved my piano to the new house while Daddy Fletcher was at the laboring yard. But soon as it was settled safe and sound in Hugh and Mamie's living room I had worries.

"What if Daddy Fletcher comes to take back my piano?" I asked Hugh.

"Don't you worry none about it," he said.

"But what if he stays on his losing streak and tries to sell it?"

"Let him try. Haven't you ever heard possession's nine tenths of the law?"

"What does that mean?"

"It mean 'cause this piano's at my house your Daddy Fletcher got only a one in ten chance of proving it belongs to him and not me. You know good as me a gambling man would never go for such lousy odds."

What Hugh said made a lot of sense, which eased my worries some.

From then on I didn't go to school much. It wasn't the same without Miss Milholland. But I worked like a lumberjack at my piano playing. The piano became my school and I learned new things from it every day. And Hugh was a jazz player to boot. I couldn't get much luckier than that I figured. Living in the same house with a jazz player almost made up for not having Max around anymore. But not quite.

32

Lovie Austin

May 8, 1923 was my thirteenth birthday and Hugh came home earlier than usual. I was at my piano practicing when he jaunted in the door beaming with excitement about something.

"Look at you, woodsheddin' away at that piano, Mary Berry," he said.

I stopped playing a minute and looked up at him. "Woodshedding? What does that mean, Hugh?"

He grinned. "It mean you practicing real hard, like crazy even. And that's good." Then his grin spread even wider. "I got a surprise for you, Mary Berry."

"What, Hugh?"

"Lovie Austin, the greatest lady piano player in the world, is gonna be in town next week with her band. I'm gonna go hear her and I'll take you along if you want."

My heart went a-leaping and hopping. "Where's this Lovie gonna be playing, Hugh?"

"At a theater over on Frankstown Avenue, the one that books all the best colored acts. Got music there gonna make you smile and forget all your troubles."

"Where's she come from?"

"All the way from Chicago. She's famous for writing and conducting the music for her shows."

I'd never been to a real live music show before and didn't have a notion what it would be like. When we got to the crowded music hall I clung to Hugh's hand and strained my chin into the air to try and see what was going on. Hugh fought his way through the crowd, dragging me along, till he found an empty seat. Then he let me sit on his lap so I could see better. What I saw made my mouth fall open. You can imagine my shock and thrill to see a colored lady sitting in the orchestra pit with five music players that were all men, like she was in charge. She looked so bold, with her legs crossed and cigarette in her mouth. But what was most amazing was how she played the piano with her left hand and wrote music with her right hand—at the same time! And boy was she a master at conducting that little band of players.

I'm going to be like that one day, I thought as I watched her. I felt so lit up inside I must have glowed like a lightning bug. That Austin lady never left my memory. Back home in bed I had visions all night of her in that orchestra pit working her magic.

The memory of Lovie Austin's magic almost made me forget about Max. But not completely. I still missed Max a heap and there were days I couldn't stop thinking about him.

33

Fats Waller

Turned out Hugh was full of surprises. A couple months after he took me to see Lovie Austin he came home with a beautiful wooden cabinet in the back of his pickup truck.

"Come on over and help me carry this thing in the house, Jim!" he hollered to our next door neighbor.

Mamie'd gone out a few minutes before. She had a baby on the way and her belly was feeling poorly. Morning sickness she called it and the July heat sure didn't help none.

"I need to get out," she'd said. "I think I'll take a walk over to Mama's house."

"You should try Nanny's special tea concoction for stomach misery," I told her.

She said she would and asked if I wanted to come along.

"Thank you, but I believe I'll stay here and practice," I said.

Much as she wanted to get me out of the house she was feeling too sickly to argue. So she went on without me.

Now I stood by the window and watched Hugh and Jim lift the cabinet from the truck and lug it into the parlor.

"Let's set it over here by Mamie's sewing table," Hugh said.

The cabinet was made of the shiniest wood I'd ever seen. It was wide with a curved top and doors on the front. There was also a crank on the side which reminded me of the cotton gin Grandpa told me about.

"Thanks, Jim," Hugh said after he caught his breath. "You'll have to come over after I get this thing cranked up and listen to some mean stride."

"I'll surely do that," Jim said. He smiled and nodded at me and tipped his hat. Then he took off his hat and scratched his head. "This here contraption looks like it cost an arm and a leg, Hugh. Whud you pay for it?"

"The price was two hundred fifty dollars."

Jim whistled. "That's more money than I ever seen!

How'd you afford it?"

"I bought it on time. Ten dollars down and ten more each month for the next two years."

"That's a long time to be paying, Hugh. I sure hope you can keep it up, what with that new baby coming. Well, I'll be seeing you all."

"What in the world is this thing, Hugh?" I asked soon as Jim was out the door.

"This here's a Victor Victrola phonograph, the very latest model." His face glowed with pleasure.

"You mean the machine that plays music off those metal disc things?" I'd seen phonographs before at some of my customers' houses but those had all been table-top boxes with big horns sticking out of them.

"Yessiree, Mary Berry," he said.

"Where's the horn?"

"The horn's inside the cabinet, so's it don't stick out like a big old sore thumb. Like I said, this here's the newest, grandest model they got."

"What happens if you can't keep up the payments?"

"I reckon they'd come and take it back to the store and sell it to somebody else. But that's not going to happen, Mary Berry. 'Cause me and my band got gigs comin' out the kazoo for near the next two months. The money's gonna be rolling in."

He gave me his brightest smile and ran his hand over the cabinet's shiny surface. "Just look how this wood shines. It's solid mahogany. And all the hardware's plated with real gold. Is that quality or what?"

I walked over to look at the cabinet more close. I didn't care about the wood or hardware. I just wanted to know how it played music.

"Where do you put the discs?" I asked.

"Let me show you how this rascal works. The man at the store explained it all to me." Hugh lifted the middle part of the curved top. "See this round flat thing? That's the turntable, where the record goes. And this long gadget is the tone arm, which a needle attaches to."

"What's the needle do?"

Hugh grinned at me then ran back out to his truck, grabbed a shallow square shaped box along with a smaller box, and rushed back inside. He put the boxes on the table by the Victrola and folded back the lid on the big one. Inside was a stack of discs each in its own brown paper case. He slid the top disc out of its case and placed it on the turntable. Then he opened the smaller box which was filled with sharp little metal things. He took one out and hooked it onto the end of the tone arm.

"Look here real close, Mary Berry. See those grooves circling all around the disc? There's music recorded right into 'em. This here needle tracks those grooves and sends the music clear through the tone arm and into the horn underneath. That's how you hear the music. Just listen to this."

He turned the crank a few times and the turntable started to spin. Then he laid the needle in the record's outmost groove real careful. First there was a hazy swooshy sound. Then music started to play. It was piano music and it sounded kind of muffled but my jaw dropped and I gasped in amazement all the same.

"Who's that playing?" I asked, breathless. It was the happiest, jumpiest piano music I ever heard.

"This here's who's playing." Hugh closed the record box lid and on the front was a picture of a very fat young colored man. But you hardly could notice his fatness for the huge grin on his face which was about the jolliest grin I'd ever seen. Across the box was written in big white letters: *FATS WALLER Birmingham Blues / Muscle Shoals Blues.*

"What do you think of Mr. Thomas Fats Waller, Mary Berry? This here's his very first record, hot off the press."

"I can't believe his left hand notes, Hugh. His hand must have the power of a steam engine!"

"That left hand style's called stride piano, the best piano playing there is. Just listen to him vamp at that piano. He's the bee's knees, ain't he, Mary Berry?" Hugh started to snap his fingers and do a lively two-step.

I felt a warm thrill inside and did the same. Hugh took my hand and we got in rhythm with each other.

"How old's this Fats, Hugh?" I asked as my hips

swayed and my feet slid to and fro.

"About eighteen, I hear. So you best get hustling, Mary Berry. You only got five years to catch up to his playing."

I believe Hugh was at least half joking. But I was sure I'd catch up a lot sooner than that.

FATS BECAME MY NEW INSPIRATION. Here was a real live young man not much older than me who already was famous with his music. And his music sounded so new and different. I loved Fats's boogie-blues style and worked hard at getting that magical feeling in my own playing. His powerful left hand and the jumpy happy melodies his right hand played made me want to pratice all the more. I listened to Fats every day then sat at the piano and tried to get that big full sound like he did. He started me on the road to thinking and playing strong like a jazz piano man.

And as I woodshedded more and more people would stop by to listen. Neighbors mostly but also people that just happened to be passing by. Even truck drivers. They'd all go wild when they heard me play, dancing on the sidewalk like they were at some night club. They'd even come up on the front porch and watch me through the window. That's 'cause I'd started playing with a strong left hand like Fats and that was considered amazing for a girl to do.

Folks kept telling me I played like a man which was quite a compliment. Nothing was worse than being told you play piano like a girl. Nobody thought girls had any power. Especially colored girls who were supposed to spend their whole life keeping quiet and pleasing folks. And girls weren't supposed to play jazz. A fool idea I aimed to change.

So I practiced and practiced playing my left hand louder than the right like Fats did on the record. Soon I started to realize why he did that. Because that's where the rhythm and the feeling is, like a drum keeping a steady beat. Like Grandpa's heartbeat. And like Max's.

But just like Grandpa and Max, Fats soon faded away along with my inspiration when a man from the store came to take back the Victrola. Repossessed was what Hugh called it. The store repossessed his Victrola because he was buying it on time and couldn't keep up the payments. That was a problem but the worst problem was no more Fats. The cover of my Fats Waller record box still showed Fats's smiling face but the records inside the box sat silent. So did the music inside me.

34

KDKA Radio

I didn't have to do without Fats for long since Hugh soon bought another new contraption—a radio. Such a time we had listening to what come out of that box. In Pittsburgh we were lucky 'cause we had our very own radio station KDKA. Besides Fats, my ears drank up all the fine jazz players they broadcast like Louis Armstrong and Fletcher Henderson.

I 'specially liked listening to Ma Rainey and Bessie Smith. My what singing. Made me wish I could sing like that. But instead their heart-tugging blues sang through my fingers. And could I ever make a piano sing after listening to those gals' bluesy tones. Then there were the dance tunes. The Charleston, foxtrot, and shimmy. What the blues ladies' voices did to smooth out my playing, those dances bounced it right back up again. Hugh's new radio gave my fingers more of a workout than they'd ever had. The piano keyboard was like a dance floor and my fingers were the dancers.

You'd think all that dancing would have cheered me up. But Mama had been acting peculiar which got me worried. When I went home to visit her she was real polite in a scary kind of way. She'd look at me in a way a mama just shouldn't look at her daughter.

I had a notion why and I didn't like it. My notion told me Mama was trying hard to make nice 'cause of the money she knew I could earn with my piano playing. But I didn't care about money anymore. Used to be I thought the money I earned would make Mama see worth in me and make her love me. But it didn't. The only reason she abided my visits now was because she hoped I'd come to bring her some money. Soon I stopped going home to visit at all.

The night after my last visit with Mama the Good Spirit came to me in a dream. He didn't talk to me in words exactly but through sounds and feelings. He made me see that even though my life would always be hard, things would come out for the best if I kept at my music. It didn't matter what people thought. Even what my own mama thought. If I kept doing what I knew was right everything would turn out fine. That dream gave me such a peaceful feeling and made me want to go right to the piano soon as I rose from the bed next morning. I went straight to the parlor and woodshedded away at that piano and no matter how much I practiced I felt like it wasn't enough. There was always more work to do.

"MARY, WHY YOU WORKING SO HARD?" Mamie asked as her feather duster swooped across the top of my piano. Her belly was big with the baby but she never let up on her house chores. "You been at that piano all day without a bite of food or even a sip of water. Why don't you go outside and breathe some fresh air like the other kids?"

I glanced out the window. It was Saturday and boys and girls were out on the street playing tin can hockey, laughing and whooping in the crisp October air. Part of me wanted to join them but my shyness wouldn't let me. The wild ways of the neighborhood kids scared me. It was safer at my piano.

"Go on out," Mamie said. "It'll do you good."

My eyes turned away from the kids and I blinked at the afternoon sun streaming through bright colored tree branches. Red, yellow and orange leaves danced so graceful on their gentle fall to the ground. Just like the dolls in my special song. Thinking about my Doll Dance got my fingers itching to play. My eyes drifted back to the piano keys.

"I believe I'll just stay inside and practice," I said quiet-like.

Mamie shook her head and went back to her dusting. "I don't know. I just don't know about you, Mary," she muttered.

She fussed like that sometimes about my piano playing but not in a mean way. It wasn't my music that fretted her but me being in the house all the time and not playing outside with the other kids. But that's the way I liked it.

Truth was my heart still ached 'cause I missed Max so much. He promised he'd write but he hadn't yet. That had me worried. What if I never heard from him again? What a burden that would be on my aching heart. I wondered if even my music could heal a hurt like that. I couldn't stop thinking about how it felt to have Max's arms around me, how strong and comforting those arms were. I wanted so much to feel all that tingly happiness again. I'd write to him myself if I knew where to send the letter. All I knew was he and his mama were somewhere in Philadelphia. Clear across the state.

I tried hard as I could to put Max out of my mind by thinking about Fats Waller. About his music and how it got me playing piano like I never had before. I couldn't listen to his records but I could hear him on the radio or in my own head. And that playing in my head poured through my fingers till I felt like I was bursting from the inside out. If only I could hear Fats play for real. Now wouldn't that be something.

Even with my head full of Fats's music my pining for Max didn't let up much. But as the weeks went by I had less and less time for it. Mamie was fixing to have her baby around the New Year and it was all I could do to help her with chores and keep up with my practicing. When the baby came early and never stopped crying Mamie and Hugh were right grateful for my piano playing. Every time I played my Doll Dance song for the wailing little thing she quieted right down. Mamie and Hugh were real beholden to me. Hugh even decided to go out of his way to encourage me in my music.

35

Jazz is Love

I about fell over when Hugh told me the news.

"Fats Waller's coming to town to play piano for a weeklong show, and Leonard Harper the club manager's hired me to play sax with the band!" He'd just run in the door all breathless. I'd never seen him so excited.

But his excitement was nothing compared to how I felt. My heart near jumped right out of me. "Oh Hugh, when's he coming? Do you think I could go with you one day that week to meet him?"

"Hold on, Mary Berry," he said, trying to catch his breath, "let me answer one question at a time. First off, he's coming right soon, the day after Christmas. And yeah, I'll find a way to get you in somehow."

"What do you mean find a way to get me in? Won't the show be at a regular theater like where we saw Lovie Austin?"

Hugh moved closer to me and hushed his voice. "No, not exactly like that theater. The place Fats is playing at is really a speakeasy, which means folks drink booze there even though the Prohibition's outlawed it. You need a password to get in."

"A password? What's that?"

"A secret word that tells them you're not a cop trying to sneak in and bust the place."

"Oh." This speakeasy place sounded a little scary, but I knew it would all turn out fine long as Hugh was with me. And I'd do about anything for the chance to meet the real live Fats Waller.

Hugh and me took the trolley to the speakeasy the very first day of Fats's show. The night air was shivery cold and there was even a few snowflakes starting to fall. I stood with my hands stuffed in my coat pockets, bouncing up and down to get warm while Hugh told the man at the door the password. He leaned close to the man and whispered so I couldn't hear, seeing as I had no business knowing about how folks secretly got into such places. That's what Hugh'd said to me on the trolley. Well whatever the secret word was Hugh whispered, the man at the door let us in.

Fats was easy to spot. There was no missing him. He was so big he about filled the place. But his face didn't look jolly like on the record box. He sat at a table spread with music paper and watched with a real serious look on his face while Mr. Harper rehearsed the dancing girls.

Hugh grinned at me then winked and went off to get set up with the band. I stood staring at Fats, afraid if I opened my mouth all that would come out would be one big stutter.

Finally Mr. Harper yelled, "Okay, Fats, we're ready! Write us some tunes for this dance number!"

Fats started writing with a fury and it seemed he'd never stop. He must've composed six tunes while he sat there at that table. Then he went up to the bandstand where the piano was and played all this new music for Mr. Harper. I never heard such playing in my life.

I snuck up closer to watch his hands. He was wild. He was all over the piano and it seemed the piano didn't have enough keys for him. Truth was it scared me to watch him. So I closed my eyes and listened real hard. And a strange thing happened. Just like when I was three years old and watched Mama play the pump organ, I could hear what note Fats was going to play next. Like telling somebody's fortune. Then I could see what I felt in my heart and I knew what was happening with Fats's music. I guess my gift of seeing gave my mind and ears a fastness in that way.

Soon as Fats stopped playing Hugh went over to him and pointed at me. "See that little girl down there? She can play everything you composed today."

Fats looked down at me from the bandstand then broke into a merry laugh. "Go on from here, man! You telling me this little gal can play more than Chopsticks?"

"Can't nobody play piano like Miss Mary here," Hugh told him.

Fats grinned his big old grin. "I don't believe it. Come on up here to the piano, Love Bird, and show old Fats what you can do."

I about froze from fright but somehow I made my way up to the bandstand and sat at the piano.

"Okay, Love Bird," Fats said, kind of snickering but friendly. "Let me hear those little fingers make some big sounds."

I looked up at him. He was smiling at me in a charming way, like a great big roly-poly little boy. I felt so tiny next to him. I put my fingers on the keys, took a deep breath and started to play. I don't know how but somehow, like magic, I played everything I'd just heard. My favorite was the one Fats called "You Take It From Me and I'm Taking It To You."

After I finished I looked up at Fats again and he was still staring down at me. Only now his charming smile had stretched into a huge grin. He picked me up right off that piano bench and swooped me in the air. "You smash those keys near hard as I do, Love Bird!" Then he put me down and looked at Hugh. "Where'd she learn to play like that? You teach her?"

"No, she learn by herself. Don't need no teacher training, that one."

"Just like me, I guess," Fats said, grinning down at me again. "That's how I learned, teaching myself. And you play like me, Love Bird, always playing your left hand louder than your right. That's where the beat and the feeling is, you know, in your left hand. Just like keeping a steady drum beat."

I didn't tell him I already knew that. But my shyness eased up a little and I grinned back at him. Fats understood exactly what was happening with my music, like I understood what was happening with his.

Then he did something that almost made me fall on the floor. He told Mr. Harper to hire me for the week. He wanted me to play that very night while people were coming into the speakeasy and finding their seats. Before the band and Fats started their show.

My heart thumped with such a commotion. But there was no time for jitters. People were already starting to stream in and sit at the little tables that were scattered around the room. And Fats had disappeared somewhere to get ready for the show.

I sat at the piano and played without fear during the audience's settling down time since everybody was talking and drinking and not really listening. After a time, I don't even know how long, Fats came out to the piano and everybody in the room stood up, clapping and cheering. I scooted on down to one of the little tables fast as I could and joined in the clapping. Then I sat and watched Fats do his wonders. I couldn't keep my toes from tapping the floor and I think if I could've listened to Fats all night my toes would've kept right on tapping.

Suddenly in the middle of his piano antics Fats turned his head and looked right at me with his big sparkly grin. "Come on up to this stage and show these fine folks how you can play piano to beat the band, Miss Mary!" His roaring voice sailed through the big hall and hundreds of pairs of eyes turned to me. I about keeled over.

"Get yourself right up here, Lovebird!" he yelled again while his magical fingers kept vamping away at the keys. "Show'em how the little piano girl can smash these ivories hard as a man!"

My belly did a somersault. Then another one. Could I do this? I forced myself to stand and start walking up to the bandstand but my knees were shaking like flimsy tree branches in the wind. Maybe I'd wither up and blow away like a dried up leaf was all I could think. Least that would save me from looking like a fool on that stage. But I was no dried up leaf. I was a girl all full of life and music and things to show people. I couldn't just blow away.

Soon as I got to the stage Fats stopped playing, stood up, grabbed my hand and pulled me onto the piano bench. My fingers were shaking but I started to play my favorite song, "My Mama Pinned Rose on Me." Before I knew it Fats was on the bench beside me playing one of his roaring strides underneath my steamy blues tune. With Fats at my side I was so filled with boldness I felt like lightning bolts were shooting through my hands. My fingers kept moving and my heart kept drumming. Fats and me played and played and my oh my what a time we had.

The audience went wild, cheering and laughing. Everybody was on their feet dancing and having a ball. When Fats and me finally finished, both of us panting and sweating and grinning, the people in the audience clapped and whooped like they'd never stop.

AFTER IT WAS ALL OVER and I was stepping down from the bandstand who should I see but Amy Frank, looking all brazen with her short blond hair and even shorter dress. A regular flapper.

"Well!" she said, standing right in my way so I couldn't get past her.

I stared at her red lips. The lipstick was painted on in kind of a heart shape that made her mouth look higher up but smaller somehow.

"How'd you get in here?" I asked. "You got to have a password."

"My friend's big brother got us in," she said with her chin up. "He's a regular here."

I was in no mind to listen to the mean things I knew she was fixing to say.

But she surprised me. "You were fabulous."

"I was what?" I could feel my mouth hanging open.

"You know, really nifty."

I looked into her painted face. There was no terrible smile. Now her smile seemed friendly and real.

"I just want to say how swell it is to know you, Mary," she chirped.

Even my second sight couldn't tell me if she really thought it was swell to know me. Or if she just wanted her flapper buddies to think she was friends with a jazz piano player. It didn't matter. The Good Spirit had put the Ghost Dog to rest. I didn't need Amy's approval. But I sure did appreciate her kind words.

FATS HAD ME PLAY PIANO with him every night that week. I hoped Mama would come to hear us but she didn't and neither did Nanny. Daddy Fletcher came one night and I almost cried when I saw him. The tears that wanted to come were happy and sad at the same time. Sad because things had changed between Daddy Fletcher and me but happy because I couldn't forget how he bought me my very own piano and taught me about the blues. His kindness had helped make the music inside me come alive and that would never change. Least not in a bad way. I knew deep down in my bones music could only change my life for the better.

I wished Max could have been there. But him not being there didn't hurt near so bad as I thought it would. I thought I needed Max. Now I knew I needed music more. Especially jazz because now I knew what jazz meant to me. It was my bridge to other people's worlds. And to their minds and hearts.

That week I learned the real value of something else Max and Daddy Fletcher taught me. Jazz is love. And love doesn't keep people apart. It brings them together. When Fats, Hugh and the other musicians would come out to the bandstand and touch their instruments I could feel that love. And that love was for everybody. It felt like being part of a family and I knew the Good Spirit was at the heart of that family feeling.

The power of the caul, the veil that kept me separate from folks since the day I was born, was nothing compared to the power of the Good Spirit. The Good Spirit had used my gift of second sight and the music in my head to bring jazz into my life. And I knew jazz would always be my most faithful friend. It would live in my heart forever, and it would save me.

Author's Note

Over the next couple of years, from age 14 to 15, Mary had the opportunity to meet and perform with jazz superstars Duke Ellington and Louis Armstrong. In 1927, at age 16, she married saxophonist John Williams, and took on the name "Mary Lou Williams" as her professional name. She went on to a successful career in jazz composing and performance, working with most of the great jazz musicians of her time.

Mary experienced a spiritual conversion during the late 1950s and embraced the Catholic faith. For the next twenty years she devoted much of her time to charitable works and composing sacred music. She even composed a jazz mass that came to be known as "Mary Lou's Mass."

In 1977 Mary was invited to become Artist in Residence at Duke University, in North Carolina. There she taught jazz history until her death, from cancer, in May 1981, twenty days after her 71st birthday.

Acknowledgments

There are so many whose aid and support helped make *Jazz Girl* possible. I'd like to thank Linda Dahl and Dr. Tammy Kernodle for their excellent biographies on Mary Lou Williams and for graciously consenting to read my late drafts. Many thanks also to advance readers Louanna Sowa, Finnbarr Dunphy, Raphe O'Geaney, Trilby Plants, and Anthony Dowd for their very helpful input. And a special thank you to Mary's longtime friend Rev. Peter O'Brien, S.J. for his many words of encouragement.

I am especially grateful to Mary Lou Williams, and the wonderful, revealing writings she left behind about her life, music, and insights on jazz, in particular *My Life with the Kings of Jazz*, "Music Can Help Youth," and "What I Learned from God About Jazz."

Go to

www.belcantopress.com

to see photos of Mary

and hear her music

CPSIA information can be obtained at www.ICGtesting.com
Printed in the USA
LVOW11s0844010215

425218LV00002B/483/P

9 780615 353760